DARKNESS RECLAIMED

10 TALES OF EVIL PERSONIFIED

Authored By

DAVID FEULING

JUDITH FIELD

GRANT HINTON

JOEL HUNT

KIMBERLY REI

MICHELLE RIVER

J.M. SMITH

K.T. TATE

MARK TOWSE

TOR-ANDERS ULVEN

Darkness Reclaimed

Paperback ISBN: 978-1-7770410-6-9

Cover designed by Michelle River
Compiled and formatted by Michelle River

We want to take a moment and thank you for purchasing this book and supporting Eerie River Publishing, and our indie authors featured.
Don't forget to read all about our authors in the "About the Author" section at the back.

When you are finished reading this collection of stories please take a moment and review it on Amazon, Goodreads, and/or BookBub.

Don't forget to check out our other titles available through Eerie River Publishing at
https://www.eerieriverpublishing.com/

Available now
Storming Area 51: Horror At the Gate
Don't Look: 12 Stories of Bite Sized Horror

Coming Soon
Forgotten Ones: Drabbles of Myth and Legend
It Calls From The Forest
It Calls From The Sky
It Calls From The Sea

List of Stories

The Itch

By: Mark Towse

Joe sighs loudly and turns onto his back after kicking the freshly washed duvet from the bed. He studies his fingernails for blood and skin, but the only blood he finds is dry from where he bit the nails down yesterday. The fresh cool new territory of the bottom sheet provides temporary relief for his back, but the unreachable prickling is soon making its presence known again. He digs his fingers into his chest to gouge at the latest and most intensive itch, but he can't fool the brain—they are like stumps—no sharpness at all.

He convinces himself there are thousands of tiny bugs crawling over his skin, and he can't bear it anymore, so starts roughly scratching at his back again. It's worse than yesterday, much worse. Images of them laying eggs and defecating on his skin fill his head, and he's sure they must be breeding. For the second night in a row, he is still awake past midnight, and he is on the verge of tears. His head begins to itch—that has never happened before. They are spreading fast. The fingers of his right hand provide momentary relief on his scalp, but he feels as though he is chasing the bugs around, and they are constantly moving just out of reach. His back is8 getting worse, and the fingers of his left hand are doing nothing to stem the itch that seems to be burrowing further into his flesh.

At work yesterday, he had wanted to say something, but how do you begin to talk about a skin infection with work colleagues. Besides, it was year-end—people had called in sick, and everyone else looked stressed and too exhausted to care.

Later that evening, he had phoned his parents—his dad suggested it might be dermatitis, but right now, it seems much more serious than a simple skin allergy. The soonest the doctor could see him was next week; they were apparently short-staffed and incredibly busy.

He feels as though his skin is alive—a hypersensitive composition of raw nerve endings that are randomly making their presence known. The back of his neck is next, and he moves his right hand to chase that one down, but it quickly moves just out of reach again. He moves his left hand from his back and across to his right thigh as a new patch of skin cries for attention. There is yet another outbreak near his ankle and then the latest and worst of all, on the bottom of his foot. He begins hitting it with a closed fist, but it does nothing. There are new patches of torment everywhere, and Joe begins to punch himself on the back of his neck, scalp, spine, and legs.

He assumes the bed is teeming with the microscopic bugs, so he jumps out, and in a frenzied state, starts brushing himself down.

There is some relief to escape the sheets that must be by now a writhing landscape of infestation, but he can still feel them on him, and worse—in him. His boxers and T-shirt, he throws into the bin next to his bed.

The remote control on the floor catches his eye, and he quickly grabs it, shakes it, and then switches on the TV. The noise provides a brief slice of normality to proceedings but doesn't detract from the escalating intensity of his itchy skin that is demanding his complete attention. Words fill the room, but most of them cannot be heard above the thoughts in his head that are screaming at him to scratch some more. He hears something about the third day as he slides open the window and enjoys the hit of the cool breeze as it caresses his body, but the relief is temporary as he starts to claw at his skin once again. The sound of sirens can be heard from all directions, and from his tenth-storey room, he notices the blur of lights against the backdrop of darkness.

He can hear the whir and chopping noise of the helicopters, and above the sirens, he thinks he can hear people screaming. And was that gunfire?

For just past the midnight hour, the night is abnormally explosive.

Every square inch of his body then sings out in a chorus of irritation. He rushes towards the bathroom and catches the words "Emergency Broadcast" as they scroll across the bottom of the TV screen, but takes no heed and quickly steps into the shower and turns the tap. The immediate hit of cold water catches him off guard, but he welcomes the brief override of the maddening itch. He scrubs at his skin relentlessly with the sponge, but he can't get deep enough.

The itch manifests in his eyes next, and he digs the balls of his hands firmly into his sockets—they squelch like marshy ground as he rubs frantically. He fumbles at the shower door and steps out of the water, watching himself in the bathroom mirror as he rakes at his chest and back. His skin is red and flared, and his eyes bloodshot and puffy, underlined by huge dark circles. In frustration, he screams and punches the mirror. It fractures, sending shards to the floor. The sensation is unbearable now and getting worse. He picks up a piece of glass, and there is immediate relief as he runs the sharpness across his chest and back. But it's not enough, and he can feel the inward retreat of the alien bodies inside him.

There is a scream for help down the hallway, but Joe has other things on his mind, and he pushes the sharp edge of the glass into his chest. The skin concedes and a small lake of fresh crimson forms. He follows the itch around with the blade and buries it deeper. His reflection makes him feel sick, so he returns to his bedroom, working now on his wrist. They are definitely in there; he can feel them. As the blade digs in further, there is an explosion of pain. His overloaded nerves cause him to let out a piercing scream. His body seems to vibrate with agony, and it is seconds before it stabilises to a dull but painful throb. They move again, and he stabs himself in the leg multiple times and then in the centre of his left hand. The TV is droning on about a terrorist attack and something, again, about the third day, but he needs to get out of the apartment into the cold night air. His skin is on fire.

He swings the door open and catches sight of a naked lady slumped against the far wall—multiple gashes and fresh glistening blood decorate her body. One of her eyes is leaking, and some implement remains buried in its corner.

There is a smeared line of blood across the elevator button. He presses it multiple times with his good hand, leaving his own bloody trace. A scream emerges from one of the rooms behind him, followed by a loud crashing noise against the door. He hears footsteps and then another thunderous smash, as though someone is throwing themselves against it, or someone else.

Finally, the lift arrives, and the doors open to reveal two more motionless and naked bodies—one half of a pen emerges from one of their necks.

As he steps in, the glass in the elevator reveals the full extent of the damage he has done to his body. Still, the intrusion marches on, and it feels now as though something is gently gnawing at his spine.

The elevator door opens to a cacophony of screams and gunfire. There are naked and half-naked bodies every-where strewn across the floor, each of them torn, bloody, and lifeless.

Near the reception desk, he sees two men merci-lessly beating each other, but they are pleading to be hit. Their naked bodies are covered in red patches, and their faces swollen and bloody.

Joe makes a run for it. He has no plan as he brings the glass into his right thigh but feels that if he can make it outside, there may be a chance of salvation. He sprints to the foyer door, thrusts it open, and gives himself to the coldness of the night in the hope it will somehow cleanse him.

As he stands there naked with the shard of glass still sunk into his thigh, there is a scream from an ap-proaching soldier wearing a sinister-looking mask. "Get down on the floor!"

But Joe doesn't get down to the floor. Instead, he breaks down in tears and screams at the top of his lungs for the soldier to shoot him. More gunfire punctures the air, and he closes his eyes, but the impact doesn't come. The soldier with the gun is still aiming at his head.

The soldier looks down the scope. The order was to shoot on sight. He wasn't trained to shoot innocent civil-ians; they should be going after the terrorists, not cleaning up their mess.

Their brief was so limited, just that people were going insane—killing themselves and each other. The scientists have no breakthrough yet.

The bleeding man before him is begging to be shot, but he can't bring himself to pull the trigger. He wonders what his father would do or what his family would say if they knew he was aiming his weapon at the unarmed man. He immediately releases his right hand from the gun to attend to a sudden itch and slakes his fingers across the back of his neck. As he does, he watches the man retrieve the glass from his leg and plunge it into his eye. He doesn't stop there and continues to stab himself multiple times on all parts of his body. The screams are unbearable. The soldier places his hand back, steadies the gun and fires off a shot that is a direct hit between his eyes. He watches as the man falls to the ground, still clutching the glass.

There is an immediate and intense itch on the soldier's cheek, but he can't get to it because of the gas mask. The night continues around him, but his part in it is over as he sits down in the middle of the road amid the chaos and begins to cry. The itch is driving him crazy now, but he still dares not remove his mask in case of infection. He couldn't bear to go like the man he had just shot.

Shadow Games

By: Kimberly Rei

She stood statue-still, looking down on the freshly turned dirt. Everyone else had left and a light rain was starting to fall. She wrapped herself in her own arms and allowed a twist of a smile. Jesus, this was something out of a bad movie. If she listened carefully, there was probably imploring grieving music playing in the background somewhere.

For years, decades really, she had waited for this moment. She'd dreamed of it. Planned for it. What would she do when he was finally in the ground? She would spit on his grave, of course. Maybe piss on it. She'd raise a drink to his soul burning in hell. She'd dance and leave her footprints on the coffin. She'd rage and scream at him, saying all the things she never had the courage to say when he was breathing.

And here she stood, statue-still, looking down on the freshly turned dirt. She was alone. No one would stop her from doing everything she had fantasized about.

She couldn't move.

Nothing she did now would matter. If she'd found the nerve to pick up the phone, just once, and tell him what he'd done to her. If she'd bought the damned plane ticket and looked him in the eye while she laid out her nightmares for him to drown in as she did every night. If, if, if. What good would it do to say it now to soil and the satin and wood prison that held him?

Tears filled her eyes and dragged her back through the years to a concrete room painted concrete gray. It was not a welcoming place, but it was her last salvation if she would only close her fingers around the hand held out to her. He'd tried so hard, that nice man in the official uniform. The patches on his arms and the badge on his chest promised to save her. They promised her a life away from the hurt and shame and confusion. The proof in his hands was damning but not quite enough. He needed her to say the words. He'd been begging her all summer long to talk to him. She might have, if they hadn't sent her home at the end of each meeting.

Home with one who didn't wear a badge and hadn't promised anything. Home, where she was too stupid to function and too worthless to live.

In the cemetery, she flinched. Memories shouldn't have this kind of hold. All the self-help books talked about taking your power back but it was all too easy to get tangled in the bear trap of the past. Truth or not, she'd learned to believe him. And because she believed him, she let him touch her. Be quiet now. There's nothing to cry about. He loved her and he was trying to teach her. Stop crying, damn it, or he'd give her something to cry about.

And then he did.

She scrubbed her fists over her eyes, grinding away the tears. The grave came back into view and with it, some semblance of balance. Would the dreams stop now? She'd sacrificed a great deal to be here. To watch them cover him in foot after foot of heavy dirt. She hadn't told anyone where she was going because she didn't want their sympathy. Time off from work with no explanation. Friends worried that she suddenly had to go out of town. A baffled fiancée who only said, "I'll be here when you get back." Even if she'd managed to stammer out her reasons, they wouldn't understand. How could they? They loved her and when you love someone, you're there for them in these trying times. The books told her that as well. But she didn't want the hugs and understanding. She didn't want the shared rage. She didn't even want the paid time off. It would all imply that he meant something to her.

The rain had become a downpour, soaking her to the bone. She was wet and cold and clammy all the way through. The mound of soil in front of her was turning to mud and slithering down. She stumbled back, not wanting it to touch her. A burst of superstition convinced her it was tainted. Her black boots slipped and she threw an arm out to catch herself. A strong hand gripped her, steadying. She looked up to offer thanks and nearly swooned in terror.

He smiled down at her. He was taller than she remembered. Taller than he should be. Hell, he should be in the ground. She shook her head in wild denial and pulled on her arm, feet sliding again on the uncertain soil. His grip only tightened.

"Miss me, babygirl?"

She tried to speak. Her mouth opened and closed. Opened and closed. Her gaze darted around, frantic for a visual touchstone to break her from this hallucination.

She was back in their old kitchen, his fingers twisting her arm as he waved a fork in her face and screamed about the speck of a water mark marring a tine. She was lazy and useless and he was going to teach her a lesson. Again.

Her boot slid. He hauled her against him and wrapped an arm around her waist. She could feel him, firm and warm as he hugged her close. She could smell his cheap aftershave and the pipe he smoked most nights.

The top of the stairs now, cringing as he beckoned her to his room. For a nap. Just a nap, he promised. But it was never just a nap and while he was asking and not demanding, she knew the price of denial.

Rain ran down her back, chilling her skin. He brushed a kiss across her forehead and gripped a breast, too tight, too cruel. "You've grown up, babygirl. What do you say? One more time?" His hips ground against her and she could feel his excitement.

Dragging out the wrestling mats. She'd done something wrong and now she had to roll around with him, pretending he was giving her a chance to fight for herself. He'd laid out the black bra and panties on her bed. She had better lingerie than any of her friends. When she dressed and went to face him, he told her to take off the bra.

He was turning her, pushing her back against a thick tree. The branches offered some cover from the rain, but no protection from him.

A thousand dollars held out before her. No? Two thousand, then. Two thousand to wrestle him fully naked. There were things he could teach her, he said. Things every young girl should know going to their wedding night and why let some fumble-fingered boy try and guide her? She'd looked at the money and actually considered it. Two thousand dollars at age sixteen. Surely she could run away on that. He would wear her down eventually and when he did, this offer would be gone. She told him no and endured two weeks of constant abuse for her sin.

His hand groped at her coat, trying to open the buttons and move the fabric out of his way. He seemed even taller, looming over her.

No choice this time. No cash. No question. Just taking and taking and taking. Later, she would paint a different picture of her first time. For too many years, she would believe it herself.

The coat parted and he groped. One hand gripped her throat and lifted her off the ground, choking her as he reached between her legs. She kicked, but her flails went through him, his flesh turning to smoke where she assaulted him. Steel where he held her.

She stood over him as he slept on the couch. The gun lived in a leather holster, hanging from his bed's headboard. Now it lived in her hand. She held it to his head, all too ready to pull the trigger and end this. He didn't so much as stir. She could do this. He deserved it, didn't he? Thoughts of more police and arrests and jail clogged her mind and froze her finger. She stood there in a cold sweat, desperate to destroy him. But no matter how hard she tried, her hand wouldn't obey her. She didn't pull the trigger. She couldn't do this after all.

He had her. He was stripping her and she couldn't fight him. Again and again, he had proven that she couldn't win. She lost every battle with him until she finally learned to stop trying. Only when he had fully broken her, when she had nothing left to lose, when she was on the verge of opening her wrists one sobbing summer night did she find the courage to run. By then, she'd been eighteen and in college and he couldn't legally stop her. But he'd never left her. Over the years, he whispered of her worthlessness. He was waiting at every failure. He invaded her dreams until she, who had not attended church in years, stumbled to a pew to pray for his death. Only then would she be truly free.

She didn't pull the trigger.

Or so she thought.

She didn't pull the trigger.

The world began to fade into shadow and darkness. It licked at the edges of her vision. Air was becoming a precious thing, leaking from her and refusing to return. She batted at the arm holding her up, only to encounter more smoke. Long lashes slid down, too tired to care anymore. The child within stood in the concrete room. She went home and endured. She cried. She begged.

And then.

And then.

She pulled the trigger.

He vanished in a puff of acrid soot, filling her lungs and blinding her. When she stopped coughing, she was once more alone. The clouds parted, allowing a shred of sunlight to creep through. Her throat hurt and her clothes were a mess, but he was gone. She rose from muddy knees to stand once more over the grave. One last glance at the headstone and she turned her back on it, a whisper of derision trailing behind her as she made her way home.

"Beloved Father, my ass."

The Extra Channel

By: Michelle River

It started as a little bit of harmless voyeurism, a silly guilty pleasure that I thought I would get bored with or feel guilty enough to stop. Instead, I found myself obsessing over the little screen and the beautiful woman with the long black hair for weeks, secretly wishing I could become her, even just for one day.

What would lead me to wish that you ask? Well, the short answer is motherhood. You see, eleven months ago my twins were born and although it was the happiest day of my life I was ill-prepared for what happened next. I love my boys, they are the fire that sparks my soul and the reason I do anything, but life as a mother was much harder than I had imagined. The first few months were rough, to put it mildly. I had a fair helping of post-partum, issues with breastfeeding, and then the soul-crushing guilt when we switched to formula. Top that off with feeling like my body wasn't mine anymore and less than three hours' sleep a night and I was a wreck, and so was my marriage.

So when I put the boys down for their nap that day two months ago and the video monitor beeped alerting me that there was movement on the second channel, I hit the button without even thinking. It didn't occur to me at that moment in time that we didn't have a second camera and hadn't even used the second channel before. Like everything else in my life, I was just doing what the little screen told me to do.

And there she was, in full HD glory: a beautiful woman with long flowing black hair like a young delicious Penelope Cruz, perched on top of a slate grey counter, silk floral robe draped across her shoulders, and legs spread wide. Her back was turned towards the camera, which was angled high above the small eat-in kitchen giving a full view all the way into the open-planned living room. I could see her writhing, her head falling back as she arched her body, her black hair cascading around her. I would like to say that in that moment I had no idea what was going on, but I did. I had seen that look before; hell I been that young woman once. Full of sexual desire and vitality.

She lay fully down on the counter giving a clear view of a man between her thighs, her legs wrapping around his shoulders as her fingers gripped his wavy hair. One of his hands reached up, grasped her exposed nipple and began to play with it, tweaking it as the rhythm of his mouth consumed her. I watched with bated breath as her thighs clenched around his head and she cried out in pleas-

ure, her body trembling around his. To my disappoint-
ment, there was no sound filtering through the speakers,
just the crystal clear video feed.

I sat motionless, mouth agape, too shocked to make
a noise. I didn't want to move for fear of losing the feed,
or missing what would happen next. I watched as he
slowly stood up. Wiping his wet mouth with the back of
his hand he positioned himself between her thighs, spreading them wide for him. He was gorgeous, tall and thick in
all the right places. Like a lumberjack wet dream.

I watched as his hand moved downwards, cupping
her sex as he reached for the fly on his jeans.

A high-pitched wail broke my trance, which was
soon followed by a second cry. I switched the monitor
back onto the first channel which showed both boys sitting
up in their cribs, playing with their toes and garbling back
and forth to each other. I evaluated the situation and decided I probably had ten minutes max before all hell broke
loose and I had to grab them. So I quickly hit the button
and switched back to the second channel, hoping to catch
the rest of the show. The screen was depressingly void of
the couple, leaving me with only a glimpse of a large man
in jeans and heavy work boots walking out of frame down
the hallway. It looked like Penelope and her man had decided to make their way to the bedroom for the rest of
their encounter. I sighed. It was for the best I suppose, the
boys were ready to get up and I still had to clean up after
lunch and get dinner together. Not to mention three loads

of laundry to fold. I didn't exactly have time to sit here and spy on strangers, no matter how much I wanted to.

For the next eight weeks, I watched the video feed of Penelope. in her silk robe, entertain men one after the other. There was the burly man on Wednesdays that had a mop of red hair and a hipster beard that liked to fuck her from behind on the same counter on which I had first seen her being eaten out by Friday's man. He liked it rough and by the looks of it, she didn't mind. Monday was my least favourite, that was the man in the suit. He would come in and stand in the living room facing the kitchen and have her undress him, shoes first, but always leaving the tie on. She would then walk him down the hall like a dog on a leash and disappear from view. Day in and day out, like clockwork, there was a new man for every weekday. I had counted eight in rotation, with the exception of boots. Boots was present in every single episode I had watched so far. I had never seen his face, however, and he always seemed to avoid being fully in frame, never showing up until the room was clear of both Penelope and her daily lover. In my mind he was her pimp or her bodyguard. Always there watching, just like I was. Hidden in the background, unseen but always there.

I am ashamed to say I found myself staying around the house more often than not, doing indoor activities with the boys instead of going to the park or running around the backyard. Never wanting to be too far away from the monitor and somehow miss an episode, like it was a pornographic soap-opera and I was its biggest fan. I went as far as buying a small blow-up ball pit that fit perfectly in the living room so the boys could play in it safely and entertain themselves during the times I couldn't get them both down for a nap when it was time for my show to start. I learned pretty quickly that the channel went live around the same time every day, at 2:05 p.m. on the dot, which made it easy to plan our schedules around showtime.

Strangely enough, with the added pep in my step, my marriage started turning around for the better as well and my husband Mark noticed. After a long night of kinky adult play where I had pulled out some moves I had seen Penelope and Friday's man use, he finally got the nerve to ask what had gotten into me lately. I joked and said "You have," and gave him a silly smile, trying to brush the question off with a joke. But he wouldn't relent, and I found myself realizing the reason I hadn't told him was because I had kept this little dirty secret for so long that I felt guilty. Yes, I felt bad for spying on this person and invading her personal privacy, but as silly as it sounds it was keeping this secret from Mark, my partner of ten years, that was making me feel awful. I was so embarrassed.

I told him all about it, every sordid detail of what I had seen over the last two months. To my surprise, instead of being disgusted he seemed interested, excited almost. He asked to see for himself. He was a little disturbed, however, that our monitor was picking up someone else's feed. You see, we don't have a monitor that connects to the internet; it isn't a "smart" monitor that you can view on your phone or from a website. It is radiofrequency only, for the exact reason that we don't want anyone to be able to hack into the monitor and spy on our children. I shouldn't be able to see someone else feeds, just like they shouldn't be able to see mine. It is on a totally unique frequency. Mark went into a lot more detail, but I wasn't really listening because I had already grabbed the monitor, planning on showing him the second channel feature. Although the light wasn't on, I figured I could flip over and at least show him the kitchen. But when I turned it on I was surprised to see not only could I not access Penelope's kitchen, there was no second channel feature at all.

I was alone in the kitchen with the boys having lunch the next day when the light flashed again, letting me know the second channel was working. Confused I checked my cell, the time showing 1:02 p.m.. That was earlier than usual for the second channel to be live, I thought. The boys were safely buckled into their high-chairs eating leftover spaghetti and peas. With a lunch like that it always ends up turning into a messy art lesson where I let them play while I finish up dishes, so I figured there was no harm in giving myself a break while they played and ate.

I grabbed the monitor and hit the button, making sure to move the screen away from their little eyes, and the second channel lit up the screen. It was exactly as it had been for the last few weeks, and I let go a sigh of re-lief and made a mental note to tell Mark it was working again.

Penelope was seated on the far corner of the screen, lounging in a luxurious rose printed high-backed chair in her living room. The kind you see in magazines but would never actually buy. She was wearing the same silk floral robe she always wore, her hair tousled as if she had just gotten out of bed.

I shook my head, laughing at the fact that I was sit-ting here spying on this poor woman who was just hanging out at home doing nothing, when I saw her jump up from her seat and race towards the kitchen and out of view down the hallway.

I jerked up in response, sitting higher in my chair and leaned in towards the monitor until I was only inches away.

Moments later Penelope raced back into view, she looked frightened, her eyes wide and her mouth opened in a silent scream. She moved below the camera, out of view. I could only assume there was another row of counters along the wall, because when she emerged back into frame she was holding a large butcher knife. She held the knife in front of her, her arms shaking as she gripped it in both hands. For a moment it reminded me of a cheesy 90's hor-ror movie, where the lead sexy lady stood her ground against the serial killer. But this was no movie.

A dark shadow filled the hallway, inching closer and closer to her until a large form emerged. It was a man. I had seen him before, or at least glimpses of him. That was Boots, her bodyguard that was always around. I could tell by the giant work boots and frayed jeans he always wore, the only actual part of him I had fully seen before. He looked different from what I had imagined, his face was clean-shaven with small deep-set eyes, his features strangely round, almost feminine. Far less intimidating than I expected for a bodyguard. But why was she terrified of her security guard? Maybe he had to take care of a rowdy "John" and she was worried the other guy would get in past him? He moved another step towards her. She stepped back, mirroring his movements. I could see her face now; she was screaming at him, waving her arms frantically, the knife in her right hand as she used her left to point towards the door. Yelling at him to get out. But he wasn't leaving, he was getting closer.

He leapt towards her, his body moving much faster than it should have, knocking the knife easily across the room and out of reach. When he reached her his body had shifted, morphing during the short distance into something I had never seen before. His back bent at an impossible angle, his clothes ripped away as his body doubled in size. He became a beast of pure muscle and sinew, his old skin slopping away in a wet pile below him, like a snake shedding its skin. His head reared back, mouth reticulated open like that of a python as he stretched to his full height at least eight feet tall, almost hitting the ceiling. I could see horns emerge from his skull like a ram and he breathed heavily, his chest expanding with every breath.

She didn't wait for him to finish his change. She bolted towards the sliding-glass doors, trying to wrench them open, but they were locked. She fumbled for the latch but gave up as the thing started towards her, and ran past it just in the nick of time, barely escaping its taloned clutches as it landed against the doors only a second behind her.

She raced into the living room, grabbing a marbled Buddha statue off the coffee table to use as a weapon. It pursued her, only steps away. She quickly jumped onto the high-backed chair. Turning quickly she launched herself at it, wielding the statue above her head and bringing it down, hard, on its skull. Had it been a normal man that would have killed it instantly, but this wasn't a normal man; it was a beast. A silent scream filled the room; even without sound I could tell it was filled with rage and terror. The beast reached out just as she turned to flee towards the hallway. It grabbed her shoulder and violently tossed her into the large entertainment center along the wall, her body smashing through the glass panels and falling to the ground below. Splinters of wood and broken glass were strewn throughout her hair and along her body. I saw her try to get up, her right arm limp beneath her.

I had seen enough; I needed to do something. I grabbed my cell and frantically called 911, shocked that the time only read 1:07 p.m. Had it really only been five minutes since this all began?! I mentally prepared myself for what I had to say. I knew I couldn't tell them what was happening, they would think it was a prank call. But I could let them know someone was being violently attacked.

It took a moment to explain the situation to the operator, but thankfully he did not question why I was able to pick up a neighbouring security feed on the baby monitor. He told me they would send over an officers to my house immediately to view the monitor themselves. I just had to wait. I stressed how urgent it was, hoping that the sound of sirens would lure the beast away but knowing in my heart that they wouldn't make it in time to save Penelope.

Panic gripped my voice as I watched the beast begin kicking her with a force that sent her tumbling towards the kitchen and closer to the camera. A pool of blood stained the white marble tiles in the living room, its heavy boots leaving large bloody prints behind it. It picked up the fallen statue, raised it over its head and brought it down hard.

Forgetting my children were blissfully playing in spaghetti beside me, forgetting that I had the phone still gripped in my hand, I screamed. I couldn't hear the sickening crunch of her skull caving in beneath the weight, but I felt it. My whole body reacted as I watched her body twitch in a dance of death. It was then something happened that I cannot explain, and I will never forget.

The beast stopped dead in his tracks, looked up at the monitor, and smiled. At me. Before I knew it, the beast moved, too quickly to track on the screen. The next moment its face was all that I could see. Large yellow eyes, with pupils like a five pointed star, looked at me through the monitor. It stayed like that for three seconds, face splattered in Penelope's blood, wickedly smiling at me. And then it spoke.

I may not have been able to hear it, but I understood it nonetheless. It was clear as day, its voice echoing in my mind as if it shouted. "I can see you Elizabeth. I am coming for you next."

I sat there terrified, too afraid to move. I could hear the voice on the phone asking if everything was ok, but I couldn't respond. What could I say, that there was a monster watching me through a camera in a dead lady's apartment? No. I did the only thing I could think of. I hung up the phone, grabbed the boys, and got the fuck out of the house. Thank God Mark always makes me keep a fully stocked diaper bag in the car with changes of clothes and diapers because I didn't even think. I just ran.

I have been on the road for hours, and I just stopped for gas and a much-needed coffee. The boys are still passed out in their car seats, covered in dried spaghetti but safe for now. I haven't even dared to call Mark yet. I am too scared he won't believe me and demand that I come home, but I can't do that. Not with that beast after me. Even if it means doing this alone.

Which brings me here to you. I am looking for someone that might have some information, someone that knows what the fuck this thing is and how to kill it for good. Because there is no way I am going to let that thing get near my boys, not even over my dead body.

Death and Rabbits

By: Joel R. Hunt

When I was growing up, being the Easter Bunny was a death sentence.

You see, Easter wasn't originally about chocolate. It wasn't about eggs or rabbits or fluffy little chicks. Easter was about the torture, death and resurrection of God's only son Jesus Christ. To some Christians, the very existence of the Easter Bunny is nothing short of blasphemy. And my parents did not tolerate blasphemy.

Father in particular resented what he saw as the distortion of the holiday. He took it upon himself to create a new tradition just for our family; one that would ensure, for the remainder of our days, that we could never think about the Easter Bunny without also thinking of the execution of Christ.

Before I go into more detail, you need to understand that my Father was a twisted fucker. He never showed his children any love or emotion, he told us at length and in detail about how we were on our way to burning in Hell for all of eternity, he beat us for laughing or playing or just generally acting like children. He saved the worst of his beatings for Mother, which happened in front of us and seemingly at random, but don't feel sorry for her. She was just as cruel. At least Father gave us the courtesy of avoiding us as much as he could, spending his time out in the woods or in the barn with creatures who didn't cry when he struck them. Mother, on the other hand, felt it was her Christian duty to oversee her children at all times. She was the ever-watchful eye of the household, ready to dole out harsh punishments for any perceived transgressions. While Father used his fists, Mother had a variety of implements that she enjoyed using on us. Well, perhaps 'enjoyed' isn't the right word; I don't think she enjoyed anything. I can't remember her smiling once throughout my entire childhood. But the implements satisfied her. Canes. Belts. Fire pokers. Anything that would beat the message of the Lord into us.

To make matters worse, both of our parents rejected modern medicine. I never saw a doctor in that household, nor a dentist, nor a chemist. Mother and Father believed solely in the power of prayer. I had to watch several of my siblings die from what I now know were completely curable illnesses or injuries. Mother would be at their bedside praying day and night, and we would be beaten for not joining in, but the moment my brother or sister – their child – died, Mother and Father would simply bury them and move on. They took the lack of recovery as being God's judgment. In their minds, our prayers went unanswered not because the prayer was impossible or unnecessary, but because the child wasn't deserving of God's mercy.

After the death of a loved one, a normal family might say that "they're in a better place now," or "they went home to God."

Not the bastards who brought us up. Whenever one of our siblings passed away, their response was:

"The Devil took them back."

That was my childhood. That was the only life I knew until I escaped years later. But I'm getting ahead of myself. First, you should know about our Easter Bunny tradition. We kept a variety of animals on our land, all horribly mistreated and underfed. The most unfortunate were the rabbits. As I said, Father bore a particular resentment towards rabbits, because he felt that the very concept of the Easter Bunny was an insult to our Lord. So he found a way to punish them – and us – while drilling in what he saw as the most important lesson of Christ's life: We are all sinful, and we must all suffer for the Lord.

Each year, Father would march us out to the rabbit hutch and force us to choose one of them to be the Easter Bunny. At first we used to pick our favourites, but we soon learned better; in later years we would choose the scrawniest rabbit we could find, vainly hoping that the ceremony wouldn't last as long for them. Once we'd made our choice, the newly-declared Easter Bunny would be taken to a special spot in the garden. We would all be forced to sit in front of a small, wooden structure, with Mother standing behind us to ensure we watched. Then, reciting Biblical verse from memory, Father would thrust the rabbit against the wood.

And crucify it.

Did you know rabbits scream? They're normally so quiet, it catches you off guard. A shrill, shrieking wail. Every year I hoped I'd be ready for it, but every year it cut to my core. One nail through the first paw. One nail through the next. One through the legs.

Then we watched, and waited. Waited until they died. Sometimes they'd last half a day, but even when my youngest siblings were crying from cold and hunger, we were forced to watch until it was done.

Afterwards, the sacrificed rabbit would be taken down from its cross, and my Father would lead us to a narrow cave at the edge of the forest. There he would place the rabbit's corpse, and the cave mouth would be sealed with stones.

Three days later, on Resurrection Sunday, the whole family would march up to the cave and kneel, with Father leading us in prayer. We would ask God to forgive us of our sins, and to share with us His glory. When we had finished, Father would remove the stones one by one, and a true miracle would be revealed to us:

The Easter Bunny would be inside the cave, alive and well.

As a child, this brutal ceremony was softened by the magic and wonder of the rabbit's resurrection. It was proof to me, and to all of my siblings, that God was real, and that He worked through Father's hands. Of course, as an adult, I know better. I know that on the morning of the third day, Father would find a similar-looking rabbit, head to the cave before us, and replace the mangled corpse with a living copy, sealing it back up for us to find later that day.

Looking back, I'd like to say that this ghoulish Easter tradition was the worst thing my Father did. But it wasn't. The worst thing was what happened to Joshua.

Joshua was one of my younger brothers, and he was always a little different. Joshua cried when nothing was sad, or laughed when nothing was funny. He struggled to use words, but grunted and groaned almost constantly. He never fully learned how to use the toilet, even with Mother's increasingly vicious beatings after each accident. Any other family would have known that Joshua was disabled. He wasn't a bad child – far from it, he often surprised us with his kind and gentle nature – but he was different, and for our parents that was unforgivable. In his final few years, I don't recall Mother even calling him "Joshua". He simply became "the Devil's child".

One winter's night, something unusual happened. Father announced he was taking Joshua to work with him. This had never happened before, not for any of us; Father hated spending time with his children, and work was his escape from us. Yet for Joshua, it was the most exciting development in his young life. He hugged Father and let out a kind of moaning squeal. Father grabbed Joshua's wrist and pulled him through the door. I watched them go. When they walked out of sight, I ran upstairs and watched from my window, tracking them past the barn, through the fields, and into the woods.

For hours, I waited. I whispered with my brothers and sisters about what they could be doing out there, even after Mother caught us and beat us for keeping secrets from her. For once in our lives, we were excited for Father to return from work.

He came back home that evening.

But Joshua never did.

I realise now, of course, that Father killed him. It seems strange that there was a time I didn't know that. It's incomprehensible to me that none of my siblings, not even Mary, the eldest of us, once considered contacting the authorities. We knew Father was a monster. We knew what he did to defenceless rabbits. But as a child, the realisation that he was capable of murdering his own children was just too much of a leap for us. I think, deep down, I was still trying to convince myself that Father was a good person.

My parents never acknowledged what happened, and all of our questions about our missing brother were deflected or ignored. His name was never again uttered by either of them, and soon we stopped asking as well.

We stopped asking, but not thinking. I lay awake for countless nights wondering if Joshua was still out there, cold and alone. If he was dead, I wondered whether God would take pity on him - like he did on the Easter Bunny - and bring him back to life. I wondered if there was anything I could have done to have saved him.

But Joshua's death does not lie with me, nor with any of my siblings. That sin lies squarely at the feet of my parents. Yes; both of them. Make no mistake, Mother knew exactly what was happening. She resented Joshua every bit as much as Father did, seeing him as some kind of personal failure on her own part. I told you she was a cold bitch. She never loved a single one of us.

I finally got out of that wretched house when I was sixteen. I packed everything I had into a rucksack and walked out in the middle of the night. I left a note for my remaining siblings, but nothing for Mother and Father. I didn't care what they thought about me leaving. I was just glad to be rid of them.

I travelled as far away as I could go and set about starting a new life for myself, far away from the hell of my childhood.

I never once dreamed I'd be back there ten years later.

It was Mary who brought me home.

Her letter arrived one morning, explaining that Mother was on her deathbed and unlikely to survive the week. A doctor, of course, was out of the question, regardless of how much Mary tried to pressure our parents to change their minds, so Mary had little choice but to reach out to us. She felt, regardless of our history, that children should be there for their parents' final moments. She always had been the most responsible of us. It came naturally to her, given that she was the only real care-giver me or my siblings had in that house. As the oldest child, Mary was the one who provided comfort and guidance. Mary was the one to bandage our wounds and teach us the difficult words from the Bible. Mary was the one who advised us when to own up and accept punishment, and when to bury a secret and never speak of it again. One of my brothers, Paul, is only alive today because Mary forbid him from ever mentioning his sexuality to our parents. I have no doubt that Father would have done to Paul what he did to Joshua, rather than allow a gay son to live.

Because of this, I had – and still have – enormous respect for Mary. That's the only reason I accepted her request. It wasn't for Mother, who I would happily have never seen again. It certainly wasn't for Father, who I doubted was any more invested in Mother's situation than I was.

When I arrived back home, very little had changed. I was pleased to see that the rabbit hutch had disappeared – the Easter Bunny ritual must have finally come to an end, given that my youngest sibling was now a teenager – but otherwise it felt like I was stepping back into my childhood. All of those horrible years came rushing back to me, and my chest tightened the closer I got to the house. If Mary hadn't been standing in the doorway waiting for me, I think I'd have given up and turned back the way I came. As it was, I couldn't leave her alone with those monsters, not even with one of them dying.

Mary thanked me for coming, and we spent some time catching up. She and Luke were the last of our siblings to have stayed at home. Rachel had run away last year and was now living on the other side of the country. Mark, we both knew, had moved out some time ago, though she'd had no idea he was in prison now. Paul was doing alright, although had refused Mary's invite to come back – he couldn't face Father again, he'd said. I could sympathise.

As it started to get dark outside, we both realised I was simply putting off what Mary had called me here for. I had to visit Mother. I stepped into the house, peering around every corner like a wary animal, but I needn't have been so cautious. Father was out working. Naturally. The old fucker had never cared about anyone else before, there was no reason for him to start with Mother dying. Mary took me to the top of the stairs, and directed me to the spare room, where it transpired Mother had been forced to sleep since her health deteriorated.

I heard her before I saw her. Through the thin walls, her shaking voice filled the hallway.

"- as we forgive those who trespass against us; and lead us not into temptation, but deliver us from evil. Our

Father who art in heaven, hallowed be thy name. Thy kingdom come. Thy will be done -"

That, Mary explained, was all Mother said anymore; the Lord's Prayer, repeated over and over again, hour after hour, day and night. I imagine Mother hoped it would secure her place in Heaven. After spending our whole childhoods telling us how easy it was to be cast into the fires of Hell, perhaps she was getting nervous.

I entered Mother's room, and the person I saw lying on the bed was a shadow of her former self. Her eyes were white and sightless. Her hair was thinning and grey. I could count her ribs beneath the stained white dress she lay in. As she spoke the Lord's Prayer, her head tossed from side to side, as if she was trapped a nightmarish sleep she couldn't wake from. It was the most frail – the most human – I had ever seen her.

Mary explained that I'd arrived, but Mother didn't appear to notice. She continued her recitals of the Lord's Prayer without pause. As I stood there, Mary excused herself to prepare dinner, and I was left in the awkward position of being alone with Mother as she rambled on her deathbed. What exactly do you say to someone who helped destroy your childhood? What words of comfort can you share with a monster?

In the end, I said nothing. I simply watched her as she tossed and turned on the bed, droning out a prayer that wasn't being answered.

It was almost a relief – almost – to hear Father arrive downstairs. I waited until Mary called me down, then joined them at the table. Luke, my youngest brother, greeted me with a smile. Father ignored me. Stubborn bastard. He was thinner than I remembered, and his eyes appeared sunk into his face, but he carried that same imposing aura that I feared as a child. I had planned to challenge him about Joshua, but seeing him again in that moment, I admit I didn't dare. I took my place as Mary dished up the meal, and then Father led us in silent prayer.

At least, it was supposed to be silent, until Father slammed his fist into the table, clattering the plates and spilling the drinks.

"Whoever is making those stupid noises," he roared, "you stop it right now, before I beat it out of you!"

None of us spoke. Mary, Luke and I shared glances, and it was clear we were all thinking the same thing. There hadn't been any 'stupid noises'. Still, none of us had the courage to openly question him, even now we were adults. Under his furious glare, we started our meals in silence.

It was a pleasant enough spread. Mary was a good cook, and I helped myself to some home-made bread with salad and slices of ham. In the middle of the table was a steaming pot of stew, and while I was eager to try some, I remember too many beatings from both parents for daring to start the main meal before Father had taken some first.

Soon enough, he stood with his bowl, picked up the ladle and dipped it into the pot.

Then leapt back as if he'd been electrocuted. His bowl shattered on the floor as he thrust an accusing finger at the stew.

"What… what have you put in that?" he cried.

Mary tried to reassure him by listing the perfectly ordinary ingredients, but he shook his head, pale as a ghost.

"There was a head…" he growled, "A whole rabbit's head. Fur and eyes and teeth…"

I felt sick. Surely Mary wouldn't do that to us? She had hated the old Easter Bunny tradition as much as I had. I couldn't imagine her dismembering a rabbit, not even to get back at Father in some way.

With Luke's help, we lifted the pot over to the sink, and slowly poured it out. Father peered over our shoulders, poking at every lump with his ladle. At last, the pot was empty. There had been nothing remotely rabbit-like inside.

Father sat down and wiped his brow.

"Are you still not sleeping well?" Mary asked him.

Suddenly, there was a cry from upstairs. Father swore under his breath and told us to "Shut her up, will you!", before storming outside. The three of us ran upstairs and into Mother's room. She wasn't repeating the Lord's Prayer anymore. Instead, she had arched her back, and her twig-like arms were flailing, trying to grasp at invisible ropes dangling around her. Mary ran to her side, and tenderly took a hand in her own. I followed suit, taking Mother's other hand. She turned her sightless eyes on us and spoke with breathless excitement.

"The gates… the gates are open for me! So bright! Do you see?"

She squeezed my hand, and I gave a gentle squeeze back. The blind, dying woman before me had done many horrible things, but I couldn't bring myself to take it out on her. She seemed so vulnerable. So frail. I'm sure that, if the situation was reversed, Mother wouldn't have wasted a second of pity on me. But I've spent my life trying be different to her, and this wasn't going to be an exception.

Mary, too, was trying to comfort her, whispering soft reassurances. Soon, Mother settled back in her bed, and a peace washed over her.

"I see light," she wheezed, "The Lord is welcoming me! Lord! Lord!"

A fragile smile grew on her wizened features - the first I had ever seen on her face - but after a few moments, it melted away. Her blind eyes flittered across the room, like a lost child in a busy street. She squeezed my hand one last time.

"Lord?" she breathed.

Then she was gone.

I don't know what she saw as the moment of her death arrived.

But I don't think it was Heaven.

That night was difficult for all of us. Father wouldn't allow anyone to be contacted about Mother's body, insisting that he'd bury her himself the next morning. It would be no different from my siblings who had passed away at home, of course, but I was a child then, and I didn't know any better. As an adult, everything about the situation seemed wrong. Surely someone couldn't just die at home and be buried in the garden? Wouldn't a doctor need to confirm it? A death certificate be issued?

I decided not to argue with Father, and when he told us all to go to bed, I agreed. My plan, though, was to wait until everyone else was asleep and then call the nearby hospital and ask them to pick up Mother's body. For all I knew, she could have still been alive and slipped into a coma or some other medical complication. I wanted professionals to be involved and confirm her death before we chucked her under six feet of dirt.

So while I sat on my bed, I listened out for any noises from Father's room, ready to make a quiet call as soon as I was certain he was sleeping.

It was about 2am when the shuffling started. Low, muffled movement, first coming from one side of Father's room, then the other. At some points it fell silent, only to be followed by a flurry of scrambling. I stepped out into the hallway, crept over and pressed my ear to his door. I couldn't even guess what he was doing in there, but I heard a quiet voice. Father's voice.

I think.

Unsure whether I should fetch Mary first, I pushed open the door and peered through the darkness inside. What I saw barely made sense to me, but there was no denying it; Father was down on all fours, half-naked, crawling along the floor. At intervals, he leapt away from invisible objects as if he were navigating a minefield. His eyes were wild and he muttered under his breath constantly:

"The rabbits… the rabbits… the rabbits…"

"Father?" I asked, "What are you doing?"

Father's ashen face turned to me, his lip trembling.

"Why are there so many of them?" he whimpered, "Why do they talk like Joshua?"

Hearing those words nearly knocked me to the floor. I hadn't heard Father speak Joshua's name since his murder. I think he sensed my shock, because he closed the distance between us and scrambled to his feet, thrusting a wild finger at me.

"You let them in here! You put them in my stew! You're doing this to torment me!"

Father raised his fist to strike me, but something caught his attention over my shoulder. The colour drained from his face.

"You…" he wheezed.

Father ran. I turned to look behind me and saw nothing but an empty doorway and a blank wall, but it gave Father enough time to hurtle down the stairs, lunge at the front door and practically fall through it. By the time I got down there, he was a good way towards the woods, being swallowed by the darkness of the night.

Luke and Mary had been woken by Father's shouting, and as they joined me downstairs, I tried to fill them in as quickly as I could. Mary took a flashlight and followed in Father's direction, calling out to him, while I stayed with Luke and checked again for anything that might have frightened Father away.

We found nothing. Mary, likewise, came back empty handed. We waited until the light of morning, and then set out as a group to track him down. For hours we searched, combing the forest and the fields, but there was no trace of Father anywhere. In the end, I proposed we call the police.

To be honest, my suggestion wasn't based on my worry for Father. Instead, it was an opportunity to finally involve the authorities in this sinister situation. If Father did return, we could say we only called them to find him, but once they arrived, we could ensure Mother's body was properly dealt with, while also filling them in on Joshua's fate. I owed Joshua that much, and I owed myself that closure.

When the police arrived, they checked in on Mother's body and informed us of the proper process for getting her a burial. She would be the first in our family to enjoy that privilege, even if she'd never know it. After that, they started a search party for Father. They advised us to contact any friends or family members who would want to help. We had to explain that there weren't any.

A slow week crawled past, and by the time Father was located, we had all come to expect the news.

The police sat us down with grim faces. They explained that his body was found in the woods far from home. He was covered in cuts and grazes where he must have run through bushes and brambles, but those injuries were superficial. His death came afterwards when, at some point in his haste and confusion, he had tripped.

And impaled himself on a tree.

Three branches; one through each shoulder, one through the legs. He was stuck, unable to move, unable to free himself or get help. They told us it had taken him days to die. I suppose I should have felt bad for him. Or, given what he put us through, maybe I should have been glad that he suffered.

Instead I just felt empty.

In the months that have followed, I've done my best to move on, put my past behind me. It's something I'm becoming used to. I meet up with Mary, Luke and Paul as often as I can, although we're all busy now, distracting ourselves from our own childhoods as much as possible. My other siblings have drifted away, and I doubt we'll ever see one another again. I don't care much, if I'm honest.

Yet when I'm alone at night, without the haste and hassle of the modern world to occupy my thoughts, I've often found myself dwelling on Father's final moments. I can't help but imagine what he was thinking as he hung on that tree, alone in the woods, the life slowly leeching from his body.

I wonder if he thought about how he spent his time on this earth.

I wonder if he thought about God. And Joshua.

And rabbits.

Dear Mom

By: Tor-Anders Ulven

I can never forget that night. Not a single moment of it. I still wake up hearing that horrid scream. I can still picture that steadily growing pool of crimson slowly inching its way under the bedroom door. I can still imagine you clearly, face frozen in shock and horror, your bloodsoaked body perfectly still on the hardwood floor. And to think, mere hours before everything was peaceful. None of us knew. Knew what opening that book would lead to.

It was Brie who found it. We were just playing around in the attic when she accidentally kicked loose that floorboard. Father had always told us to stay away from there. It was too dangerous. We could fall through the floor. Break our necks. For a moment I thought that's exactly what happened; that Brie stepped through the brittle wood, her neck snapping as she hit the floor all the way down there. But it was just a loose floorboard.

"You alright, Brie?" I said. You always told me she'd need a kind and protective big sister, so I tried my best to be one. It was hard at times, you know how she can be, but I think you'd be proud of us if you could see us now.

"Yeah," Brie mumbled, "But come take a look at this. I think I found a secret."

I carefully made my way towards her, making sure to watch my step. She was in a corner, squatting over the hole left by the missing floorboard. She reached into it with both hands and gently lifted the cursed thing out of it. I remember thinking how ancient it looked. It was torn and ragged, every page smudged and stained, like it had been passed down countless generations.

"What is it?" I asked.

"It's a book, silly." Brie said rolling her eyes.

"I know that," I said, "But what's it about?"

Brie was only eight, so she couldn't really read all that well yet. She flipped through the pages, mouthing the easy words when she found them. BLOOD. PAIN. After a while she just shrugged, and handed me the book instead.

"I don't know," she said, "But it has all these strange pictures and words in it."

The cover didn't reveal anything about its content. It was faded and grey, fairly dull and anonymous, rough to the touch. But the moment I started reading the first page I knew we had found something we weren't supposed to. Something dark and secret. Something that shouldn't be. Something we were far too young to understand.

But we couldn't help ourselves. We were just kids. Curious, stupid kids.

I find myself wondering what would have happened if we'd never found the book. How would our lives have gone then? What if we had kept it a secret, Brie and me? Would someone else have stumbled upon it years later? How would reading the book have changed them? How would it have changed us? I know it doesn't matter; that I'm just tormenting myself, but I don't think it's possible to move on without at least considering the what ifs.

I've been asked to describe the content of the book more times than I can count. I could never do it. Not really. I can remember minor details, like the ungodly pictures, or random sentences that my ten year old mind could comprehend, but I could never force myself to revisit the perversity of it as a whole. I know deep down that I can do it. I just choose not to. I believe that my ability to do this; to bury the true meaning and existence of it deep down in my subconscious, is the only thing keeping me from going insane.

And I have to hold it together. That was my promise to you. Hold it together for Brie.

We sat there studying the book for hours. I read most of it aloud so Brie could understand, but I don't think either of us truly got the meaning behind the words. Most of it was in plain english, describing heinous rituals and acts so defiled and corrupted that I had to take pauses to allow the tainted words to ease their way into my mind.

Then came the pictures. Horrible, gut-wrenching images, some of which I couldn't even stand to look at for more than a second.

Every chapter had a name. I remember that vividly. Some were strange, foreign, unknown, others I could recognize. Lilith. Her portrait is still imprinted in my mind. Whenever I close my eyes, I can see her clear as day. Wretched, twisted, horrible. She wasn't the worst, but she was the one we looked at the longest.

That's when you came, mom.

We didn't hear you. We were mesmerized by that foul book. Entranced by the blasphemous morbidity of it. So when you snatched the thing right out of my fingers I couldn't help but to scream. I didn't mean to. I think you understood that.

"Mom!" I yelled, "Why did you do that?"

You gave me a stern I'm the grown up here-look and grabbed Brie by the arm. "Didn't your dad tell you two to stay out of here?" You said. I remember I shrugged and reached for the book. You yanked it away and pointed to   the   stairs. "Dinner. Now. Daddy's running late, so we'll just have to eat without him today."

We gathered around the dinner table. You placed the book on the kitchen counter. Didn't even look at it. I was kinda worried. I don't know why, but it felt like we'd done something bad. And I don't mean sneaking up to the attic-bad. Something really bad.

We didn't say much. Talked about school and such. Idle talk. But then, as we were cleaning the table, your eyes fell on the book. And you opened it. The way your face changed. That's what I always come back to. That moment of shock. Your plate fell from your hands, shattered into tiny pieces on the floor. But that look. That expression.

"Wh-where did you find this?" you asked as you flipped the page with trembling fingers.

I couldn't speak. I'd never seen you like that before. I'd seen you upset, angry, disappointed, sad, scared, but not all of them at once. You were pale. Like all the blood had drained from your face.

"WHERE. DID. YOU. FIND. THIS!" you turned to us and yelled, tears now streaming down your face.

"In-In-In the attic," I muttered, "It was hidden. Brie tripped over a loose board and found it."

"I didn't mean to," Brie sobbed, "It was an accident."

You stood there, wide-eyed, trembling, crying, just staring at us for what felt like minutes. I don't know what went through your head, mom, but I'm sorry. Sorry for everything that happened. You didn't deserve any of it.

"Did you girls read it," you whispered, "Did you look at it."

I shook my head and kept staring at the floor. I didn't like lying to you, but I knew we were in trouble. That we'd done something bad. But I just couldn't understand what. Brie cried, poor little thing. She thought you hated us for it.

"It's OK," you said, "It's OK. It's gonna be OK."

You calmed down somehow. I don't know how you did it. I could never have done it. It was like you swallowed the storm, devoured it, buried it deep down. You knew what was coming next, didn't you? I think you realised at that moment what would happen that night. But you couldn't tell us.

You told us to go to our rooms. Play safe for a while. Until bedtime. We listened. Didn't want to upset you again. But I snuck down. I just wanted to check on you. I saw you sitting there, crying, too repulsed to look at the book, yet still your eyes were drawn to it. Did you consider calling someone? I've always wondered that. Why did you feel like taking this on all by yourself? I guess I'll never know.

Brie fell asleep in my bed. I drifted off soon after. Held her tight like a stuffed animal. Before that night I didn't understand why you wanted me to protect her. She could learn on her own, like I did. She didn't need me. I understand now though. There are some things, horrible, unspeakable things, that you never wanted her to see. To experience. To understand.

I can never forget that night. Not a single moment of it. I woke up hearing that horrid scream coming from your bedroom. As I approached it I saw the growing pool of crimson slowly inching its way under the door. With a gentle push it swung open, revealing you, face frozen in shock and horror, your bloodsoaked body perfectly still on the hardwood floor.

My father's corpse was a mangled mess. I don't know how many times you stabbed him, but there was a gaping hole where his stomach should be. There was so much blood. Everywhere. I couldn't move. Just stood there trembling like a leaf.

"I'm sorry, Natalie," you muttered, "I'm so sorry."

They couldn't identify all of them. The girls in my father's perverse, depraved journal. A few of them were reported missing, others were assumed runaways, but many, too many, were never identified. Over twenty total. Twenty girls raped, tortured and murdered by my father, little more than footnotes in his fucking deranged, sickening manifesto.

I think you died that night, mom. Something inside you just stopped working. I could see it in your eyes. The life that was once there didn't shine through like it used to. And every time I visited you the light had faded just a tiny bit more. Until it was all gone. And then you left us. I don't blame you. I never will.

Dear mom. I'm sorry. I'm so sorry. But you saved us. We always made sure to remind you of that, Brie and me. We will never forget what you did for us. Thank you. Thank you so much.

Rest in Peace,

Love Natalie

Telling the Bees

By: Judith Field

Mark opened the secret desk drawer and took out the ash wood wand. The warmth from the power stored in it spread through his fingers and he felt the wood throb like a heartbeat. He muttered an incantation and the wand folded into two. He put it into his pocket.

Pat was in the garden. He joined her, tucking his hands deep into his pockets against the chill. 'We've had a call-out,' he said. 'Cuddly toys manifesting in a house in Burnham.'

'Give me a moment, I've got to finish this. I want these carrots to set seed for next year.' Looking up at the sky, she sang a golden melody about honeysuckle and summer. The wind eased. He heard his own voice singing the chorus. The buzzing of bees filled the space. One circled his head three times before landing on his hand.

'That was its way of kissing you,' Pat said. 'But I'm not jealous. Bees are the world's little musicians. They love singing, and it's quicker to bribe them into the veg garden with a few verses than to grow extra flowers.' She shivered. 'What happened to the summer?'

'Gone.' He put his arm round her and looked up at the trees, almost bare of leaves. 'And where are the swallows?'

'Somewhere warm, if they've got any sense. I'm glad this job's indoors.' She bent over the carrot plants. 'Bye now, little musicians. I've got to go to work. And so should you.' She stood up. 'You've got to keep the bees up to date with everything that's going on, they easily take offence.'

They returned to the house. 'Animated toys,' she said. 'That's usually down to life force spilling over from other duality. We need to shove it back and fix the leak. Got your wand?

He nodded, and patted his jacket pocket.

'Good. Look after it. There'll be no more. Ash dieback's put paid to that.'

The house was on a new estate; a maze of streets built between the river and the remains of Wodehouse Forest, and leading nowhere. Pat and Mark picked their way along a muddy path flanked on either side by a row of terraced houses of different sizes like a mouthful of broken teeth. Each had a plot number, apparently generated at random like the lottery.

On their second pass along the street, Mark spotted Plot 16, between Plots 73 and 2. Pat knocked on the door. A man, looking about thirty, answered.

'Court and Anderson? Thank God. Come in - I'm Gerry Finch.'

They stepped inside. The aromatic smell of new carpets caught in Mark's throat. Two pencil drawings hung in the hall, 'Josh, Reception Class', written on each. The first one showed a beast resembling a wingless dragon, wearing a top hat and a cloak. A single black eye gazed from the middle of a face that had no mouth or nose. The second showed a cross between a dog and a rabbit, with a rat-like tail and six limbs. Its mouth, looking too large for its face, was filled with long pointed teeth.

'Josh loves to draw,' Gerry said. 'Teacher reckons he's got more imagination than the rest of the class put together.'

He ushered them into a room at the end of the hallway. 'Have a seat.' Mark sat on a Chesterfield sofa covered in dazzling orange leather. Gerry perched, crossing and uncrossing his legs, on the edge of a matching, eye-watering arm chair.

Pat sat beside Mark. 'Gerry?'

'This is going to sound mad-'

'Not to us,' Pat said. 'We're used to this. Lots of entities look like toys.'

'We'll try to find a way to sort it out,' Mark said. Pat nudged him with her elbow. 'I mean, we will sort it out. Just tell us your story.'

'Moving here three months ago was meant to be a fresh start for me and Josh,' Gerry said. 'Our own garden, and backing onto a forest. I moved a couple of fence boards. Josh likes to run round in it.' He bit at a fingernail. 'It was all good, till a week ago.' His voice thickened and tailed off.

'It's OK, take your time,' Pat said.

Gerry cleared his throat. 'Those toy things showed up in Josh's room, from nowhere. Hiding under the bed.' He shuddered and a sheen of sweat appeared on his forehead. 'I couldn't catch them.'

'We can,' Pat said.

'Hang on. Things got a whole lot worse. I heard a man's voice in Josh's bedroom late one night. Went in to tell him to turn his telly off. But it was a book.'

Mark reached in his pocket and pulled out the phasmometer, a black object the size and shape of a goose egg, which detected entities. It emitted a series of staccato clicks, like dried peas dropping into a saucepan, one at a time. 'A book with pictures, you press a button and it makes a sound?'

Gerry stood and paced up and down. 'No, no. It was an ordinary book I got when I was a kid. Treasure Island. Forgot I still had it – it must be 20 years since I've looked at it. It was open on Josh's bed. He'd been drawing on the pages. The book was reading itself aloud. Stopped, when I came in.'

'Can we see it?' Pat said.

Gerry shook his head. 'I burnt it. Had to. It wasn't reading Treasure Island. It was some sort of poem, creepy weird stuff. I wasn't having Josh listen to that.'

Mark leaned forward. 'Can you recall the words?'

'Flowers...blood.' He shook his head. 'I can't remember.'

'I can.' A boy aged about four stood in the open doorway.

'Go back to your room, Josh,' Gerry said.

'No, Dad. Listen.' He looked into the distance. A dry, creaking voice came from his mouth. 'When daffodils begin to peer,

With heigh! the doxy over the dale,

Why, then comes in the sweet o' the year;

For the red blood reigns in the winter's pale,

And the sun shall flee from me in fear,

While I shall kill-'

Gerry grabbed his arm 'Shut it. That's enough.'

Josh looked at his father. 'I didn't say nothing.'

The clicks from the phasmometer changed from single peas to a harvest. Mark showed it to Pat. 'Ever seen a count rate like this?'

Her eyes opened wide. 'Some massive, unstable source of power is near, and coming closer. Getting stronger.' She stood. 'I don't think it was Josh saying that.'

Gerry let go of Josh's arm and slumped onto the sofa 'What are you on about? We all saw him.' He held his head in his hands. 'This is doing my nut in. Just go, Josh.'

Josh ran from the room. His footsteps thudded along the hallway. A door slammed.

'We need to talk to him,' Pat said.

Pat sat next to Josh on the bed. His chin resting on the drawing pad he clutched to his chest.

Mark heard a scuffling sound.

'Look out,' Josh said, curling his legs under himself, as the dog-rabbit from the drawing in the hall shot its head out from under the bed frame, nipped Pat on the ankle and pulled its head back. 'Too slow.'

'Ouch!' Pat said. 'See if you can flush them out, Mark. Then we'll zap them.'

Mark crouched by the bed and poked underneath it with his ash wand. He felt something roll away from him and edged his hand into the gap. The tips of his fingers chilled as they closed round the object.

Pat put her arm round Josh. 'It's not a very nice toy, is it?'

His face reddened and his lower lip wobbled. 'The other one's mean too. They won't let me sleep. Dad's cross all the time. It's my fault.'

Pat's voice softened 'Of course it's not. But, where'd they come from?'

'They just come. When I draw with Woodface's pencil.'

Pat reached out for the drawing book. 'Can I see?'

Josh handed it to her. She flicked through the pages, all blank.

'Can't draw any more. Lost my pencil,' Josh said.

Mark stood up, holding what he had found under the bed. It looked like bundle of twigs held together with a pencil lead in the centre. He felt the throb of a pulse deep inside it.

'Mine,' Josh shouted. 'Not yours. Gimme.'

Pat recoiled. 'That reeks of dark magic. We need to take it away with us. Start a binding ritual to immobilise it, Mark.' She turned to Josh. 'Who's Woodface – your teacher? Where did he get it?'

'Woodface lives in the forest. I didn't steal it. I found it lying by our fence. He said I could have it.'

The pencil writhed like a snake, driving a splinter into Mark's palm. He jerked his hand and the pencil fell to the floor. Josh grabbed it and ran.

They dashed after him, into the kitchen. Gerry looked up from his seat at the table.

'He's in the garden.'

Through the kitchen window Mark caught a glimpse of Josh stepping through the gap in the fence, into Wodehouse Forest. He flung the back door open and they rushed out. Turning sideways, Mark followed Josh through the gap, pulling Pat after himself.

'Wait, I'm coming too,' Gerry called. He rushed at the fence and stretched out a hand towards it. With a crack, a massive spark jumped across the gap. Gerry jerked his hand back. The smell of singed hair tickled Mark's nostrils. He pulled out his wand and used it to draw the shape of a door in the gap between the panels.

Gerry extended one of his feet. He wrenched it back again. 'I can't get through. What is it – electric?'

'Worse than that. No time to explain,' Pat said. 'You'll have to stay here. We'll find Josh.'

Pat gripped Mark's hand. A muddy path wound between the trees, through a dense carpet of dull green leaves with saw-like edges. Mark called Josh's name. No reply. Nettles towered over them on both sides. Damp air seemed to cling to the stalks. Ragged leaves hung down, patched with white as though splattered with dirty water.

Mark remembered a legend in a grimoire of Pat's. A tale of things in the woods, which blended among the trees without being seen. That you could hear muttering in the breeze, whispering to each other.

They reached a clearing, dotted with builders' rubble. In each corner stood an ash tree, bark flaking. The few remaining leaves were withered and blotched with black. Between the trees a blue-green net of power flickered on and off like a faulty lamp.

'Someone planted those trees,' Pat said, 'so that the pattern in the lines of force coming from them would keep something trapped inside. But the trees are dying and the power's failing. Something hideous has broken free.'

On the far side of the clearing stood the remains of a stone archway. As they drew closer, Mark saw that the stones that had formed its sides were carved with images of smiling, winged women with six arms, flanked by flowers. Below the waist, their insect-like bodies tapered to pointed tails.

'Nobody's done anything like this for hundreds of years,' Pat said, 'But it used to be standard practice to lock evil into the keystone, the centre of an arch, with carved goddesses standing guard.'

'It might have stood there forever. Nobody would have known, if the builders hadn't cleared the space,' Mark said.

Pat nodded. 'The ash trees, now they're something I've only read about. They'd be a back up, in case the arch fell. A back up that failed. And Josh found his way in. Over there.'

Josh sat on one of the fallen stones, drawing. They crept towards him. He looked up.

'I've nearly finished copying this picture of Wood-face. He's there, on the ground.' He pointed at the larger, wedge-shaped keystone, carved with stylised leaves, smoothed by time.

Mark looked at Josh's drawing of the leaves. At first as blurred as the ones on the stone, they grew sharper, shimmered, and regrouped into a face. The face of a man, with hair and beard made of leaves. Shoots grew out of the nostrils and open mouth.

'That's his head,' Josh said. 'I'm just finishing his body.' The pencil scudded across the page, drawing something tall and broad, with legs like tree trunks. 'All done!'

The air filled with the sound of whispering. Ivy growing on a tree rippled and turned, but there was no wind. A fern frond broke from its root with a sharp snap and writhed towards the edge of the clearing. Mark's pulse and breathing quickened. He pulled Josh to his feet. The pencil and book fell to the ground. A shape, man-like but rough-carved from lumps of wood, lumbered into the clearing, crackling as it came. It stopped an arm's length from them, its leaf-face scabbed with fungus.

'Not Woodface. Woodwose,' Pat gasped. 'Wodehouse. Woodwose. I should have known – this place breathes evil.'

Mark pulled his wand out and jabbed it forward. He flung it away as it burst into flames, burning to fine powder.

The woodwose opened its mouth in a grin, showing teeth made of jagged stumps of rotting wood. 'Ash to ashes,' it said, in a voice like twigs scraping across stone. 'Fetters of stone and ash can no longer hold me.' It raised an arm and pointed a hand knotted like a bundle of dried roots at Mark. 'Be a tree.'

Mark's limbs stiffened and locked. He felt a thrill like an electric shock running up from the earth as it rose around his feet. 'Pa-at,' His voice was slow and mechanical, like an old fashioned vinyl record played at the wrong speed 'Bind-ing...'

Pat began reciting the ritual.

The woodwose raised a club-like arm and staggered towards her. Her voice faded. 'Your words have no hold over me,' it said. 'My power is empathic. It thrives on feelings. On the fear of woman and man.' It pushed her to the ground. Her ankle bent underneath her as she fell. It moved towards Josh.

With unfocussed eyes, Josh took a pace forward.

Mark tried to cry out. His jaw locked, choking the sound into a murmur.

The woodwose turned and smashed its arm into Mark's face. 'Silence. A tree has no voice.'

Blood dripped from Mark's nose. Clear, like sap. The woodwose turned towards Josh. 'I have consumed summer. Earth will know it no more. The child awoke me. I thirst for his essence. Come.'

Tree root fingers clutched Josh around the throat. His knees buckled and he collapsed to the ground, eyes closed. A shimmering mist snaked out of his nostrils and mouth. The woodwose bent over him.

'You can't have him!' Pat dragged herself across the ground and clutched Josh's hand.

'I will devour you too, woman. But first, the boy. Younger. Sweeter.' It bent lower, burying its face in the mist.

Pat dropped Josh's hand and hauled herself to her knees. Gasping, as she picked up one of the fallen stones from the arch. Her arms shook as she lifted it and her fingers opened. It fell into a patch of mud, the winged goddess carved on it smiling up at the sky. Wings. Body like an insect. Mark willed his lips to open. He forced out a croak. 'Tell...the bees.'

Pat scooped up the ash from the burnt wand and held it in her cupped hands. She hobbled to her feet. 'Wodewose. Hear me.' The echo of her voice cracked around the clearing. The wodewose looked up. 'Your empathic magic cares about feelings. But I use literal magic. And that cares about what you do.' She flung the ash into its face. It howled, holding its head in its hands. Pat turned her face to the sky and sang 'Honey bees, honey bees, hear what I say. An evil has taken the sun away. And now I beg you freely stay. And gather honey for many a day. Bonny bees, bonny bees, save us this day.' She stared upwards. The woodwose lurched towards her.

Mark felt a stirring strength in the empty sky. A swirling, buzzing shadow appeared above them. The sound grew, as the swirl solidified into bees. More and more came, until the air was filled with the sound. The swarm covered the woodwose. It howled and keened as it hobbled in circles, beating at the bees with gnarled fists.

The buzzing grew louder. Mark heard noise inside his head, whining at a higher and higher pitch until his eyes watered and his ears rang. With a bang, like a car backfiring, the woodwose exploded into a mass of swirling dead leaves. Mark felt the stiffness in his muscles dissolve. He lifted a hand and rubbed his eyes.

Josh lay, surrounded by dead and dying bees, the mist gone from his face. Pat knelt by his side. 'It's over, Josh. You're OK.' No movement came. Pat touched his forehead. 'He's cold. So cold.'

With a cry, Gerry burst into the clearing. 'What happened?' He pulled Pat away. He laid his head on Josh's chest. 'What's wrong with him? Wake up, lad.'

'I'm sorry. We were too late,' Pat said.

'For what?' Gerry stood up, his lips curled into a snarl. 'You and your mumbo jumbo. What have you done?'

Mark dragged his feet out of the earth that had engulfed them. He staggered towards Josh, singing the last line of the incantation. All he knew would have to be enough. 'Save us this day.'

The clouds parted, letting through a faint beam of sunlight. A bee rose from among its dead sisters. It flew towards Josh. Gerry went to swat it away. Mark grabbed his hand. 'Let it come.' The bee flew in a shaky circle around Josh's head three times, before landing on his nose. Josh sneezed. He opened his eyes.

Feed Your Demon

By: K.T. Tate

I watch from the shadows as she enters the building, her chosen dwelling place littered with things that reflect who she believes she is. All the captured happy memories and colourful decoration fades away in her presence. Her aura is a blanket of dull grey, smothering everything possibly joyful in its surroundings. The photographs of her are alien now. That smile long banished. She uses them to torture herself, to show what she was and what she will never reclaim.

Slipping off her shoes even the relief of small things is lost. Her mind too consumed and exhausted to notice the relaxation of her feet, the safety of her home and the usual mundane comforts. She makes herself a cup of tea, warmth the closest thing to a positive emotion that she can feel these days. The TV flickers to life and she lets other worlds become hers, anywhere better than here.

She was beautiful once. Not in the classical sense of symmetrical features and human desirability, but in that she was happy and free. To me she is beautiful either way. But then concepts such as beauty do not have a universal rule and as such even contradiction can be maintained.

To put it plainly, something my kind is not usually wont to do, when happy she was beautiful like a sunny day and when sad she was beautiful like the dark ocean and neither of these have anything to do with appearance. But she has gone beyond sadness now and fallen into the abyss.

In her nightmares she desperately tries to save him. Yet she finds herself stuck wading through the black treacle of her own mind. It sucks her in and pulls her down until nothing but her hopelessness remains.

I wait for her to sleep. I had hoped that she would at least undress and find her bed but I should have known better. Sleeping pills, wine and the sofa have become a habit as the cold emptiness of the bed is now filled with maddening fear.

I carefully slither out from underneath the sofa, gently, tentatively coiling a tendril around her bare ankle. She does not stir as I touch her, a side effect of the pills. At least it means that I do not have to subdue her. I envelop her feet in the multihued miasma that is me and start to work my way up, forming limbs as I go.

Her clothing is no obstacle as I crawl under it where it is loose and simply soak through where it is not. Her skin and scars become known to me, forbidden knowledge inscribed on the parchment of her body. I take my time in exploring her form, careful not to pressure any point that would rouse her.

I can feel her nerves firing like a lightning storm underneath her skin, hairs raised at my presence, her body ready to recoil. Humans don't remember but the physical reaction is clear. Her adrenaline starts to flow as I caress her face, gently parting her lips.

I negate the would be terror by turning her physical attention to more carnal things, something she has been neglecting. Suckers and feelers form with ease as I manipulate her form, keeping her in that gentle, pleasurable place within the realms of sleep. Particular skills would allow me to whisper, to rouse her desire even whilst she is awake, to take part as she pleasures herself without her ever noticing as I enhance her experience and feed. Unlike certain others of my kind, it is not her arousal I am here for. Though I do find that conjoining improves the feeding experience.

But then isn't that always the way with love?

Oh yes, I love her. I cherish every moment of her bleak existence. We do not love like you love. We appreciate the brief, the inevitable, the reality of things. And right now her reality is a thick gloom, a beautiful feast that she has laid out just for me.

I gently force myself into her mouth, exploring all the damp crevices, a kiss deeper than mortals can go. She bucks slightly from the inescapable discomfort but settles quickly as I lighten my form and soak through. I coil snake-like around her energy centres. The once bright balls of energy are now dark and murky, filthy things, filled up with sorrow and loss and an anger she won't admit to herself. She is a smorgasbord of suffering.

Saving her heart centre for last I start to feed, slowly drawing out all the emotional grime. Her sorrow is like pure light, blinding and hot. Her anger a squirming struggling thing fun for me to hunt and consume. Her loss a deep rich dessert, the thick flavour of congealed blood and dying stars.

I start greedy as I have been waiting so long for this but I slow myself, savouring the little moments, taking all that she has to give me of her damaged soul and broken heart.

Pleasure, raw and physical, becomes dominant in her subconscious as I take away all other feelings leaving her energy centres grey and void. I feel the gentle rocking of her body as she sighs, a sign that I don't have long. I contemplate whether to let her climax or fall back into restless slumber.

Humans are complex things and it occurs to me that waking her with her own pleasure could cause her more turmoil, allowing her centre to refill with the conflict and resentment that sustains me. Feeding would leave her energy centres empty, numb. An absence of murk is not the same as the rekindling of colour.

Bulbous and sated I withdraw from her core. I could just phase through her but I revel in the sensation of pulling my engorged tendrils out slowly, taking my time to enjoy the warmth of being inside something living. I slink down her body, heavier than before and yet still light as a ghost. My presence like atmospheric pressure against her skin. Her flesh prickles, all the tiny hairs standing upright in protest against my caress.

I must confess that her reactions excite me, evidence that we exist together, planes merging, if only for the briefest time. And on that theme I condense down into her lap like some large cloud cat, putting effort into manifesting my already busy feelers and pseudopods. Nerves trigger and pleasure builds. Her biological song an easy tune to play and soon her body spasms, breath hitching in an involuntary gasp of ecstasy.

Her conscious mind alights and I am away. I wonder if she saw me. What would she think? That I am a cloud, a smudge, a faint shadow, or just the work of her tired brain? I wish she could see me, but I know that doesn't end well for them.

Back in the safety of the under sofa I relax, digesting. She sparks alive with confusion, disgust, sorrow. Emotions cascade, boiling up to fill the void I left. Tears bounce on the wooden floor, her wracked crying a song to rock me to sleep.

Bad Trip

By: David Feuling

It was my fifth day in Gloaming, Nevada – an un-incorporated township skirted on all sides by scorched barrenness. I had never been this far west before, and so the craggy, acacia-dotted desert was dazzling to my senses. I remember wishing that I could extend my stay, but also knew that doing so would be impossible. My business in the town was concluded, and the presentation had gone well. I was expected back at the home office on Monday.

Rather than spend my stay at a hotel, I lodged with two old friends who had moved out to the area after graduation. Jason and Clara were old sweethearts who eventually married and moved west to "live freely and without external instruction," as they often phrased it. They were glad to host me for the week, and I enjoyed catching up with them – even if they had become hallu-cinogen-fueled desert spiritualists.

I was afraid to try mescaline, and I was especially terrified to experiment with psychedelics so far away from the (relatively) settled streets and services of Gloaming. Still, Clara assured me with eager confidence that the experience would be safe as well as beautiful. "When we're way out there in the silent air of the desert," she told me, "and the peyote kicks in and there's no motion at all except for us and the campfire, all under a billion glittering stars..." She searched for more words, but instead could only smile serenely. "You'll know what I mean."

I agreed to join them on one of their "trips" before returning home.

...

That night, as we were preparing for the drive out together, Jason retrieved a glass jar with a tin screw cap from his closet, and held it up for me to see. Inside were perhaps two hundred small, clear gelatin capsules. Jason removed the tin cap and tipped several of the strange pills into his palm for me to inspect. I saw that each capsule was packed with shredded bits of something fibrous and hazel-colored. It reminded me of tree bark.

When we were ready, the three of us headed out together. Jason drove while Clara directed him out of the city, then along dozens of miles of unpaved roads. Eventually we were completely off-road, and I could feel the crags and small boulders of the landscape beneath us jostling the car as we drove. Soon Clara and Jason decided that they were satisfied by the pristine quality of the nature around them, and so Jason parked the car. The two of them set up camp while I prepared a makeshift fire pit.

When the dusk came and deepened into night, Clara lit the campfire they had built and Jason brought me my dose of peyote, along with a beer to help me swallow down the fistful of capsules. "Just eat them one by one," Jason advised. "It won't take long." He demonstrated, placing a gelcap onto his tongue, sipping his beer, and then opening his mouth to show that the pill was gone. Over by the campfire, I could see that Clara was taking hers three or four at a time, pausing only to swig from her drink.

Soon we had each finished taking our dose. We drank and watched the fire together, and waited for what would come next. At first we spoke aloud to each other while we waited, but before long we were sitting in silence. The emptiness of the desert pressed inward with a tangible urgency for quiet, and it had rendered us mute.

Eventually, I noticed that I had become raptly attentive to the campfire flickering in front of me. Prismatic streaks of color had begun to spark out from the flame and into the night air, each one cascading like a living mote of light. I felt giddy, and noticed that Jason and Clara both seemed to have entered similar states. With smiles and searching eyes, they were watching the stars.

I turned my eyes back towards the fire, eager to lose myself once again in its dazzling movement. I began to melt back into its warmth, but soon noticed in myself a strange sense that something large was moving through the darkness nearby. Turning my focus towards the motion, I saw a human shape standing alone out in the desert, only barely illuminated at such a distance by the camp-fire's flickering light. If it were only a few paces further away, I thought to myself, the shape would be completely obscured by darkness.

"I see something." I heard myself say it out loud, but my voice sounded hazy and strange. Jason and Clara lazily turned their attention towards me. With a peaceful smile, Jason spoke.

"What do you see, Vince? Describe it for us."

I strained against my own vision, which was already limited by the dark but now also warped by the peyote. Indeed, even the sand and the trees seemed to be moving and shifting around me. Still, the figure was not something abstract. It looked like a large man who was marching in place unsteadily, listing back-and-forth as he did so. It would take a step forward, then two steps back, then perhaps four rapid, mincing steps in our direction again, then another three steps back. It was staring in our direction the whole time this went on. The figure's torso bounced gently against the elastic, up-and-down motion of its knees.

"I see a person," I began hesitantly. "Or, I think I do." I shifted in place nervously and then corrected my-self. "I don't think it's a person. The eyes haven't blinked at all." Indeed, the eyes were shining bright to me, like two illuminated pinpricks against the darkness around them. They never flickered or dwindled at all as the figure marched.

"It's probably just an owl," Clara offered, her back still turned away from the thing. "Does it seem like the eyes are darting around in circles, or making shapes in the dark?"

"Yes," I replied with a sobbing sort of crack in my voice. "But see for yourself, it's not like an owl."

Clara propped herself up on one arm, and looked over her shoulder to follow my pointed finger. Her lazy smile turned suddenly into a deep frown, and I felt nauseous to see the way her face had dropped. Jason noticed too, and turned to look with the same, sudden loss of relaxation. It seemed the thing was really there.

A series of warbling, clicking vocalizations rang out suddenly from the thing's direction. As it continued, the procession of sounds grew more complex and strange, and soon the noise was rolling over itself like an ungodly, squealing battle-cry. It seemed to me that the thing was calling out to us deliberately, and this idea made my whole body tense up until I began to feel paralyzed. Clara and Jason began to shout at the form which still marched aimlessly without moving closer.

"Get lost, asshole!" Clara's voice rang out fiercely, but I could hear that she was growing afraid.

"You're going to wish you hadn't fucked with us!" Jason added, projecting his voice across the desert in a similarly unsure tone.

But the thing did not seem to mind their threats. In fact, it began to advance slowly and deliberately. Soon it was close enough to the campfire that I could see it more fully. I wasn't sure, but I felt that I could see the thing spasm badly across its whole body with every few steps that it took. It was as if the creature was struggling through some kind of grand mal seizure at it moved – and somehow it was winning the fight. In my vision and in my mind (both of which were already swimming with peyote fantasies), the thing contorted and twitched like a grotesque and poorly-directly marionette.

As it lurched unevenly across the sand, seemingly unresponsive to our shouted insistences that it leave, the thing began to click and mumble its strange sing-song noises again. This time, though, the sounds it made were more like English.

"Just get lost already!" Clara shouted, and rose to her feet to confront the humanoid creature that was now only a short distance away.

"Juss geh loss!" the creature bellowed back, and then added a hiccupping sort of chuckle that echoed softly in the night's silence. It did not slow its approach.

"Find me the car keys," Jason said quietly to Clara. "I'll scare it away."

Keys in hand, Jason moved quickly to unpack a tire iron from the trunk of the car, and then stood by the campfire with the makeshift weapon brandished over his head. "This is your last warning!" he shouted. "Don't make us hurt you!" He took several steps towards the thing, as if prepared to attack. To our relief, the creature planted its feet and stood still. Clara and I shared a glad smile before turning our attention back to Jason.

When we did, however, we saw that Jason had dropped both the car keys and his weapon to the earth. He was now walking – lazily but deliberately – towards the thing that now stood patiently in the nearby darkness. The creature, staring at Jason with its shining and seemingly lidless eyes, waited patiently for him to join it where it stood, and then seem to lead Jason backwards into the opaque dark beyond the campfire in a marching sort of dance.

It had squatted down low and craned its head forward into Jason's face; that's what I saw. It seemed to me that the creature had hypnotized my friend with its unbroken stare as it backed away into the dark. Worse still, the thing actually had to stoop down, drop its shoulders, and bend its knees before its eyes were level with Jason's. Whatever it was – it was much taller than humans generally get.

Clara and I both began to scream. We were so lost in panic that we couldn't register anything besides our own begging sobs for Jason to return to the campfire – to please, please, please come back. We howled until we were both breathless, and when we finally stopped, we felt that utter and complete silence from before pour back over the desert. For perhaps a minute, the emptiness of the place was punctuated only by the soft crackling of the fire.

Then there was Jason screaming — screaming from somewhere that sounded like it was an impossible distance away. He was crying out in the kind of frantic anguish that only comes from someone who truly can't believe the pain that they're in. I looked at Clara in wide-eyed terror, and she mirrored my expression perfectly as her head swung around to look back at me. As suddenly as they had begun, Jason's lamentations died into silence with a slushing, drowning sort of final gasp.

I was too petrified to move, but Clara was already on her feet. She hoisted me up by the front of my shirt and ran me over to where the car was parked. Before I could even fully register what was happening, she had pushed me into the backseat, and then rushed to retrieve the car keys from where Jason had dropped them on the ground. Soon she was back, sitting in the driver's seat and doing her best to start the engine despite her badly shaking hands. "Which way is the road into town?" She whispered urgently, as if afraid to raise her voice too loudly. "Which way did we come from? Answer me, Vincent!"

"Just go," was the only response I could muster. "Just get us away from here." I felt an overwhelming vertigo at that moment, as if my spirit was trying to escape my doomed body, and so I shut my eyes tightly to regain my orientation. After a short while sitting like this, I realized that Clara wasn't talking to me anymore. In fact, she wasn't making any sound at all. My head was swimming so badly that I had been certain the car had at least lurched into motion, but when I opened my eyes Clara was sitting placidly in the driver's seat of a stationary vehicle. She was staring silently through her window. As I followed Clara's gaze, I saw that the thing was back – perched on its haunches a short distance away. The illuminated orbs in its eye sockets were focused on her. It was drawing her away from me.

I pleaded with Clara not to leave me alone as she removed the keys from the vehicle's ignition and dropped them casually to the vehicle mat at her feet. She stepped out of the car and towards the creature. I stumbled dizzily from the backseat, and attempted to grab her around the shoulders. In automatic response, she elbowed me viciously in the guts and left me winded. I collapsed against the car, and when I found the strength to raise myself up again, she and the creature were gone.

I struggled desperately to get the car back into motion, but the combination of mescaline and adrenaline in my system made progress difficult. The steps involved in starting the engine, then putting the car into drive escaped me, and the lettering on the manual gearbox felt alien – as if I had forgotten the Roman alphabet completely. It did not help that as I was working to start the car, I could hear Clara's voice (always so sweet and calm before tonight) now screaming wildly with a throat that sounded choked with gore.

Clara always spoke like music: pleasant, and soft, and wonderful. What tore through the cold desert air now, though, were ragged and wordless gasps of pitiful agony. The silence that eventually followed was worse, though. It told me that I was all alone.

I turned to peer out the driver's side window from where I sat, still having failed to start the car. I could see that the creature had returned – once again lumbering playfully out from the obscurity of darkness, but this time directly towards me. I felt as if my panic would cause me to faint at that very moment, but mortal fear galvanized me to keep fighting. I finally managed to summon the engine to life, but pressing on the gas only caused the engine to rev in park. I could feel the creature's eyes on me, and I knew that it was nearly at my window. I turned my back away from the window as deliberately as I could while still pressing the clutch down with one foot, and gripped the stick shift to pull it into a new (but arbitrary) position.

My vision was swimming too heavily to discern precisely what gear I was now in, but I did not care so long as the car would start moving. I faced forward and prepared to step on the gas, but suddenly found myself staring directly into the eyes of the creature. It was perched on the hood of the car now, and watched me through the windshield with those bulb-like, electric eyes. I closed my own eyes tightly, in a final bid to resist the thing's hypnotic lure.

I was preparing myself to die, but a monstrous shriek and the sound of wild, receding footfalls broke my terrified meditation. It sounded to me as if the creature had suddenly been attacked, and was now fleeing. After remaining motionless for several moments with my eyes shut, I noticed the faint sensation of sunlight on my eyelids.

Sunrise was breaking over the distant mesas. The creature was gone, and it occurred to me that such a horrible thing could only exist in hellish darkness. For the first time since the creature had appeared, I felt as if maybe I could relax. Completely distraught, I drew the deepest comfort I've ever known from the warmth of the sunlight on my face. I lost consciousness without realizing how exhausted the night had left me, and slept for a few hours. When I awoke, I found that the peyote had mostly worn off, too. Feeling mostly sober now, I drove straight into town to find help for my missing friends.

I went to the police, and tried to tell them my story in a way that would seem at least halfway believable. I admitted everything that I could, knowing full well that it all sounded like a stereotypical "bad trip". Skeptical and more than a little annoyed, a pair of officers eventually agreed to follow me out into the desert to investigate the details of Jason and Clara's disappearance. Together we found the remains of our campfire, and a snarl of erratic tire-tracks in the sand. But there was no sign at all of my companions. Nor did the officers detect any signs that a struggle had occurred anywhere near the site.

The police soon concluded that the disappearance of my two friends was probably a simple matter of Clara and Jason having been surprised by the strength of mescaline. "They thought they were prepared by their previous experiences," said one of them, already walking back towards the cruiser to drive us into town again. "And so they trusted themselves to wander out into the night alone."

"Shared delusions are fairly common in these sort of scenarios," the other officer agreed. "You were lucky it was your first time trying this stuff. You were too overwhelmed to follow them, and so you stayed by the fire instead. That, and the fact that you sat in the car with the engine turned on until sunrise, probably saved you from freezing." He paused and raised his gaze upward, as if stopping to feel the sun on his face. "We'll do our best to find your friends out here, but in all honesty I'd be surprised if they survived the night."

...

I'm home now, safe, and far away from whatever that terrible creature was. Or at least I think I am. But I've realized something awful, and more and more the idea is driving me crazy. There's no way for me to be completely sure that I'm not still out there, hypnotized and being led to my death while the fantasy of escape goes on. Let me try to explain it a little better. Every night since I left Nevada, I keep having the exact same dream. Every. Single. Night. The same terror plays out in my mind in precisely the same way, and it always goes just like this:

I'm driving out of Gloaming. It's around noon, just after the police have told me, "We'll do our best to find your friends." I'm glad to be heading home. I consider calling my mother before I begin driving, but then realize that I don't know what I would say if she answered. I'm still shocked and exhausted, so I decide simply to make distance between myself and the town.

I press eagerly on the accelerator as I drive, and yet for hours it seems as if I can make no progress. With a creeping sort of anxiety, I realized that there has not been another car in sight for hours. Even the signage on the roadside has dwindled away to nothing. My surroundings are now like an unfinished painting: jarringly without details. This is nothing like the road on which I had originally traveled into town. I don't recognize anything.

With a suddenness that rends my heart from top to bottom, the steering wheel melts away from beneath my hands. The car, the road, and even the sun above me all dissolve in an instant.

I find myself standing in the undisturbed sands of the desert, teleported back into the almost perfect darkness of that gruesome nighttime. The creature looms and croaks a sound nearby, staring directly into my eyes. I realize that I've been looking back into its face for who knows how long. The safety of that morning's sunrise – the relief of my narrow escape – they were all simply delusions inflicted upon me to occupy my mind as I march myself towards execution. In this dream, my waking life is the fantasy. I am still out there with the creature.

The thing howls at an ear-splitting volume, and I brace my hands against my skull in an attempt to resist the sound. Still, my knees buckle and I fall to the ground. The thing is inches away now, and I can see that it draws oxygen into itself from a number of chitinous vents which dot its chest and neck. Periodically, they suck inward like gasping mouths before relaxing again.

As the thing leans in to consume me, the sounds it makes become quieter and more discrete in tone. It begins to suck air more rhythmically, and releases each breath with a low hiss. "Haaa... Eeeeeth... Haaa... Eeeeeth..." As I feel it finally touch me with its hand-like appendages, it chokes out words. "Eeeeeth... Don't you... Haaa... Miss your friends?"

With a slobbering, suctioning sort of sound, the flat and featureless jawline of the creature unfolds into a gaping maw. Chevrons of razor-edged teeth present themselves from fleshy folds all along the inside of the thing's throat (which has now spread open like the distended jaws of a snake.) Now exposed to the air, they shimmer against the blackness of the night like stars.

In this dream, I am still under the effects of the peyote, and so I see ghostly emanations of impossible color snake outwards from the creature's face and form. Quivering hallucinations pool around the thing, like lesser nightmares gathering to join it. Jeering, ephemeral demons spring through the night air towards me with each eager spasm of the thing's face. Fractals drip from its lidless eyes, and I can feel that I too am weeping.

In this dream I can't stop having, the sun does finally rise over that expanse of forsaken desert, but I am not alive to greet it.

3, 2, 1 ... Go

By: J.M. Smith

Even from an early age, we could tell Logan was different from other children. He didn't babble, make eye contact, or acknowledge other people very often, so it wasn't particularly shocking when he was diagnosed with autism spectrum disorder. I've always known the world could be a cruel place to those who learn differently, so I made it my mission to educate myself and learn the best ways to help him reach his full potential. Within a few months, Logan was enrolled in various early intervention services: speech therapy, occupational therapy, sensory integration therapy, physical therapy, and a preschool program for children with disabilities. Our time became heavily scheduled to fit everything, but, while it stressed me out, Logan seemed to thrive with his strict schedule and therapies. He started making huge gains in every aspect of his life, except communication.

It was hard not to get discouraged, what mother doesn't look forward to the day their child says "mama" for the first time? Amanda, his speech therapist, never gave up. She was constantly working on alternative communication methods in addition to speech, but none of it seemed to get through to him. It took six months of home speech therapy three times a week before Logan finally started to babble. It wasn't happening as fast as I would have liked, but it was progress. Over the next several months, the babbling became more common and Logan started to imitate sounds. Amanda was certain that it wouldn't be too long before he started repeating words, and looking back now, I wish she had been wrong.

Logan had been in speech therapy for almost a year when he finally said his first words. Amanda and Logan were working in the living room, while I was in the kitchen when I heard the sweetest sound I've ever heard; Logan said his first word, "Three." Shocked, I dropped the glass I was filling and went running into the living room, "Two." Amazed, Amanda and I looked at each other, both of us tearing up from pure happiness. The two of us had grown quite close during the past year, and I knew she was relishing this moment every bit as much as I was. Just when I thought it couldn't get better, Logan walked over to Amanda and gave her a big hug and made direct eye contact with her for a few seconds: neither of which were things he did regularly. "One". Thinking he was done counting, we both started cheering while jumping, like we were out of shape adult cheerleaders. In all the noise we were making I almost didn't hear Logan when he sadly whispered "Go". Amanda instantly collapsed. Concerned, I called out to her, asking if she was alright, but she didn't answer. She'd never answer me again.

Seven minutes. That's how long it took the ambulance to get to the house after I called 911, and I spent that entire time desperately trying to follow the operator's CPR instructions. I'm still not sure if I did it correctly, but the paramedics made it sound like it wouldn't have much of a difference. I held Logan and sobbed while I watched them roll the stretcher from the house to the ambulance. The next few days went by in a haze. I know I called Lakewood Group, the company she worked for, and my husband, Grant. Lakewood Group must have called Amanda's family, because her car was gone the next morning when I got up. Grant took a few days off to help me in any way he could; he knew how close Amanda and I were and wanted to help. He called Lakewood Group and managed to get the funeral information for me. Since Logan had never been a fan of large groups of people, we agreed that Grant would stay home with Logan while I attended the funeral to say goodbye. It was at the funeral I learned Amanda's death was caused by a ruptured brain aneurysm. Her family was surprisingly welcoming to me, especially her mother. It turned out that Amanda had frequently talked about Logan and his progress in therapy, and hearing that Amanda's last act was to help Logan speak seemed to bring some peace and comfort to her mother.

Things returned to normal pretty quickly in our house after the funeral, but that's to be expected when you have a child who craves staying on his schedule. Lakewood group found a new therapist for Logan in a matter of days. I tried to explain to Logan why he wouldn't see Amanda anymore, but I wasn't sure how much he actually understood. Even in children with typically developed communication skills, death is a complex subject for an almost four-year-old to grasp. Daniel, the new therapist, was great with Logan, but still, Logan hadn't spoken since his last session with Amanda. At first, I thought he just needed time to warm up to his Daniel, but after a month with no further progress I began to worry that he had been traumatized by the events of that day. I had spent so long waiting to hear his voice and I was terrified that I might not get to hear it again. I would find out later I was right to be terrified, I was just terrified of the wrong thing.

Saturday was Grant's birthday and we had made plans to meet with his parents for dinner. Seeing as it was a beautiful day, I took Logan to the park that afternoon while Grant stayed home to set up the new computer that I had given him.

The park was a bit busier than usual, but we were lucky and found an open swing. Logan has always loved swinging and made a beeline for the swings the second we got there. He had been on them for quite a while and there weren't many swings on the swing set, so, when I noticed that some other children seemed to be waiting for a turn, I told Logan it was time to get off. I had already begun to prepare for the meltdown that usually occurred when something like this happened, but it never came. Instead, Logan calmly walked over to the sandbox. I told him how proud I was of him for sharing and made a mental note to brag about how well he handled the situation during dinner later that night. I was sitting on the bench closest to Logan, watching the children that had taken over the swing set. They were taking turns seeing how far they could launch themselves from the swing, marking where they landed with lines in the mulch. I remembered playing games like that in my childhood, and, for a moment, the fear that Logan might not get to experience that distracted me. I almost didn't hear him. "Three, two, one...Go!"

A boy that looked to be a couple of years older than Logan had just launched himself from the swing. I don't know if it was intentional or an accident, but his body started to roll back while he flew through the air, as if he was attempting to do a backflip. I watched in horror, realizing he wasn't going to be able to make it all the way around before landing. Involuntarily, I closed my eyes as he hit the ground, but I didn't need to see it to know he didn't land the flip; the sickening crunch and chorus of high-pitched screams were enough to paint the picture. Maybe it was just a parental instinct that sent me running toward the swing set despite my modest first aid skills, but, once I got there, I quickly saw there was nothing I could do to help him. He was face down, but his body was laying across the back of his head, chest up. It was as if he had been folded over at the neck. I couldn't move, I just stared at his lifeless body, surrounded by screaming children.

After what felt like an eternity, the boy's mother had made her way to the swing set. I knew she was his mother by her anguished cry; the kind of sound that can only be made by a parent that has just lost their child. Somebody must have called for an ambulance, because the sound of the sirens is what finally snapped me from my trance. I suddenly felt like I was intruding on a private moment not meant for me, so I grabbed Logan and took him home, the sound of that woman's cries echoing in my mind the whole way home.

When we got home, I told Grant what happened at the park. He comforted me the best he could, and asked if I wanted to stay home while he took Logan to meet up with his parents. I wish I had taken him up on that offer, but I didn't want to be alone replaying the afternoon's events in my head. That evening, we all went to Grant's favorite restaurant, and I did my best to put that after-noon's events out of my mind. Grant's parents spent most of the evening encouraging Logan to speak again, but he was much more interested in eating his chicken nuggets than talking. Just when I had begun to relax and enjoy my-self, Logan started counting down again, much to the delight of Grant and his parents.

"Three, two, one...Go." Our entire table cheered for Logan, congratulating him on doing such a good job, but the sounds coming from the opposite end of the restaurant were a different kind.

It wasn't the loud, boisterous sounds that you might hear normally in a restaurant, instead it was the crashing of glass and screams of panic and shock. My head immediately turned toward the sounds, and before I knew it, I got up to see what was happening. Up until this moment, I had rationalized the aftermath of the previous times, but I knew that if it had happened again, I wouldn't be able to do that anymore. I was so wrapped up in my thoughts, I didn't notice Grant had followed me until I heard his gasp when we made our way through the crowd. My mind seemed unable or unwilling to fully grasp what was happening.

The smell was the first thing I noticed, I had never realized that blood could have a distinct smell. The copper scent was so strong, I could almost taste it, as if I had pennies sitting on my tongue. A tray full of broken dishes lay near her head, broken glass with bright red splashes, and the pool of blood surrounding her body still seemed to be growing. Several people were around her, covered in blood, trying to help. I recognized the CPR compressions one man was doing from my attempt to help Amanda, and another man was holding what appeared to be a red tablecloth against her throat. Grant took my hand and I followed him back to our table wordlessly, the whole time wondering if Logan's counting was somehow to blame for her unfortunate accident.

The next day, there was an article in the paper about the waitress. Her name was Ashton, and she left behind two little girls. I found myself feeling incredibly guilty, but decided that I couldn't confide in Grant about my suspicion that Logan's counting was somehow connected to the deaths that occurred afterward. It sounded crazy, even to me, and I was the one thinking it. Instead, I decided to throw myself into helping Logan learn new words, hoping that once he had mastered full communication this awful situation would just end somehow. But that's not how the world works. Awful, tragic things don't stop happening just because you want them to, and unfortunately for us, Grant and I would see many more awful things.

It had been a month since Grant's birthday dinner, and we hadn't heard a word out of Logan that entire time. Which is why we were both shocked to hear him while we were out grocery shopping. "Three, two, one...go." Neither of us had ever discussed our thoughts on the strange occurrences every other time Logan had spoken, but it was hard not to notice we were each nervously looking around. We exchanged a small chuckle once we realized what we were doing and that everybody around us seemed to still be going about their business. Grant took Logan over to the toy aisle to pick out a toy as a reward and I headed to the checkout. I didn't notice the commotion by the door until I was putting the groceries on the conveyor belt. I didn't need to see to know what was happening, but I felt compelled to see it for myself. I was filled with a sense of dread as I made my way through the crowd. The paramedics were already there, loading an elderly man onto a stretcher. I felt numb as I walked back to the aisle where I had left our groceries. Grant and Logan found me not too long after they wheeled the man out of the store, and Grant could tell by my face that something had happened again.

When we got home, we put on Logan's favorite movie while we stepped into another room to discuss what had just occurred; neither of us wanted to talk about what had happened in front of Logan. It was a relief to finally say out loud what had been worrying me for so long now, and even more of a relief to hear Grant had the same concerns. Unfortunately, neither of us knew what to do about it. We didn't think Logan was intentionally doing anything to harm other people, and we weren't sure if Logan was the cause of the deaths or if he just somehow knew they would happen. Both scenarios seemed equally impossible. We briefly considered taking him out of speech, but, since he mostly spoke outside of speech, there didn't seem to be much of a point. We talked in circles, but never found a solution to our unique situation.

Only a few days had passed after the incident at the grocery store, and I was taking Logan to go visit my grandmother. I'll admit, I was a little apprehensive about taking him out, but I decided I couldn't let that cause me to deprive him of the people in his life who loved him.

We left the house a little later than I would have liked, and got stuck in the after-work traffic. I was focused on driving, so I didn't see what caused it, but out of nowhere Logan started screaming his head off. He had always loved riding in the car, so I was completely unprepared for a meltdown while driving. I was trying to split my attention between calming him down and keeping an eye out for the impatient drivers that always seemed to cut into a lane at the last possible second. Nothing I said was having a calming effect on Logan, if anything it was only getting worse. He had started banging his head on the side of his car seat and fidgeting with the straps holding him in the seat.

In the rearview mirror I saw him manage to unbuckle himself, so, even though we were only two lights away from our turn, I immediately pulled into the nearest place on our side of the road. I had pulled into a gas station and parked the car at one of the pumps. I walked around to the side his car seat was on and Logan jumped into my arms squeezing me tightly around the neck. I was shocked by this random display of affection; normally he hated to be touched following a meltdown. I hugged him back, wondering what had him so out of sorts, when he whispered in my ear, "Three, two, one, go".

The sounds of screeching tires and crunching metal were deafening. I looked over and saw that a semi-truck had ran the red light causing several cars to crash. I saw half of what looked like the car that had been behind us sticking out from under the truck; the other half was crushed beneath the wheels. At that moment it dawned on me, we could have been that car had I not pulled over. I was shaking too much to be able to drive, so I just stood there hugging Logan back with a ferocity only a worried mother could muster.

During the last six weeks Logan spoke on eleven separate occasions. All of those times ended with at least one person dying, except for the time the carousel roof collapsed at the zoo; that resulted in the deaths of several children. We didn't stay long enough to find out exactly how many children died that day. Most days Grant and I handle these situations to the best of our abilities, although days like the zoo weigh heavily on both of us. We try not to let Logan see the devastation that inevitably follows every time he speaks; no child needs to be exposed to that. We don't get much warning, and we never know who will be next, but Grant and I continue to hope we will find a way to warn whoever Logan is counting down for. So far, we have been unsuccessful. That's why I'm telling all of you now. Please, if you see a child who is obviously different, don't laugh at his noise canceling headphones or whisper amongst yourselves when he has a meltdown in public, and, if he speaks, listen to what he has to say...because he could know more than you could possibly comprehend. Your life may depend on your ability to look past his differences and see the value and wisdom he has to offer.

Tunnel Vision

By: Grant Hinton

The thrum of the train tracks douses the otherwise oppressive silence of the carriage in a thin monotone drone. A sheen of perspiration coats the windows and my neck from the sticky heat of the train compartment. The headline of the newspaper in my hand flashes by as I use it as a fan while staring out the window. Boy aged four, mowed down by a drunk driver. Lush green countryside passes by like a patchy green carousel. A light drizzle zigzags down the outside of the window forming what I imagine are lightning bolts. It's befitting the dull, cloud-laden skies, and my mood. The train door hisses and cracks open. A woman wearing beige jeans, a red flannel top and tan boots enters. I smile. She returns it with a gruff head nod and then seats herself across the aisle facing the rear of the train. A wave of blonde hair conceals most of her face. I only get one blue eye and half a straight lip. She looks young except for the ton of worry that weights on her brow.

"What's with the heat, right?" I say, trying to strike up a conversation. It's like I've been sitting here forever.

Her eye flashes to mine and then back out the window. I can see the stubbornness in the set of her shoulders. Round, bunched and tight. Then her foot starts a steady rap on the floor.

Tap tap tap tap tap tap.

"You know, you're more likely to be run down from a drunk driver than be involved in a train crash?" I state, thinking the nervous tick is a phobia. She doesn't flinch. It's not like I expected a reaction. Well, I did actually. I expected her to say how she's always been scared of trains ever since she was a little girl. Some childhood accident blah blah blah. But nothing? In truth, I'm talking more for myself than anything else. Having someone listening to you can chase away most of the demons just as effectively as sharing one's pain.

"I'd ask where you're headed, but I don't think you'll tell me. Even though there's only one stop. Kinda makes me wonder why you're on board though."

The foot stops tapping, and she gives me a quizzical look. This time she holds my gaze a few seconds and then runs over my attire. The scrutiny lasts longer than I like. I find my hand going to the name badge on my chest pocket.

"Are you a Doctor?"

"Of sorts," I muse, patting the tag. "But not in a practising way, not anymore, at least." I reach into my inside pocket and pull out my flask, take a swig. Her lip curls slightly. Not a smug expression but one more dismissive than surprised. Nonchalantly she turns her attention back out the window. The rain clouds are really setting in. The possibility of a downpour is imminent.

"You got kids?" She asks in the reflection of the glass. I glance down at the bear at my side with the brown tatty fur and gently pat its head.

"For a friend," I say. She eyes the canister in my hand, so I offer her the flask.

"No! Ok then. Well, nowadays I go to conferences. Life on the road, so to speak." I waggle the flask. "Caught too many times." My light-hearted chuckle enlists another head nod.

"I'm on the way to one now actually." I bring out a pamphlet from an inside pocket as the flask disappears.

"Egotech?" She sounds surprised. "That's a silly name." She doesn't bother hiding her disdain. I retract the pamphlet and continue to fan myself with the paper. In the brief stop, I see her eyes fixed on the picture of the front page. It's a young blonde haired boy holding a teddy bear.

"That's what most think until they see what Egotech can do. You ever heard of an app called Victory? No?"

She snaps out of her reverie and shakes her head.

"Big back in the 2000s? No? Well, It was meant to get the younger generation active again, like the Pokemon go of the 2010s but more immersive. Pull them off the gaming console and mindless virtual pursuits and bring them back to the real world. And it did for a time. The idea was simple. You sign up and earn real-life rewards for defeating challengers."

The lady turns toward me, the motion reveals the start of a scar below her left eye. She quickly catches her locks and pulls them back into place. I know she's intrigued. My need for conversation has won out, so I continue.

"In the beginning, all a player had to do to win was make the other player surrender their phone. The winner would tap the surrender button and the challenge was won. Only some of the kids didn't want to hand over their phones. Lead to a few punch-ups."

"Sounds barbaric." She says, all attention of the scenery now gone.

"Have you read Lord of the flies?"

She shakes her head.

"Well, Ralph would be devastated." I chuckle again. The teddy bear falls over with my shakes, so I set him right.

"Barbarism wasn't our intention But, as time moved on it did devolve into that realm. Players took the game more seriously than expected. What we thought would be a simple game of tag turned darker. Leagues formed, regional score sheets were drawn up. Advertisement sort the more popular players. Eventually, drones followed the active hunts. Players no longer just submitted their devices after a brief scuffle. Full-blown fights took place right in front of everyone. Naturally, schools banned the app. But the mainstream ate it up. Matches were scheduled, bets took place. Single fights turned into massive battles. When the first person died, Egotech contemplated removing the platform but it was huge by them. Not just in the UK but worldwide. After the third death, Egotech decided to pull the plug, but it was bigger than us."

"How'd that work out for you?" She says smugly.

I can deal with smug, Most people are when I tell them this story. You got what you deserved often follows their triage. But she leaned in to accept the pre-offered flask. I didn't expect that so soon. I can see the tension in her shoulders lessen with the alcohol, even though her tone remains unimpressed.

"You know. I never used to drink." She says. "Couldn't stand the stuff. Now I can't get it strong enough." She laughs mirthlessly.

I retrieve the gin and take a swig. "There were a few complications I'll admit," I ramble on. "But we were lucky that all our waivers were signed. The big payoff happened when some Japanese company brought the rights to keep the app going."

"Nice company you work for." She spits.

A thunderclap sounds outside. Clouds boil over the farmland terrain and I worry about it. It's not far from us and I never like thunderstorms. I listen for the next bolt. It rings out strong. Maybe it's half an hour, or ten minutes away.

"I'm Ben, by the way," I say shaking the feeling off. My hand closes the distance between us fully expecting her not to return the favour. She eyes it like a dog would a hand with a whip in it, but reaches out. Her grip is firmer than I would have imagined but at least it a good full handshake and not one of those limp finger jobs. I hate those.

"Melody." She says. "Mel for short."

"So what are you running from, Mel?" I ask. I considered not asking it so early, but something in her eyes tells me that she wants to get something off her chest.

"What makes you say that?"

"Well, I don't see any bags," I shrug, then smile passing the alcohol back. "When people run away they do it on impulse with the clothes on their backs."

"So what are you running from then?" She asks.

I mull over the life I've lived to this point. The decision I've made. My tongue works the back of my teeth. She flicks from one eye to the next thinking I won't answer. That one deep blue eye takes me in. I can see a twist of white woven within.

"A lot of things," I say shrugging again.

I didn't realise I stopped fanning myself until I look down at the paper. I think momentarily and then continue.

"Things I can't change, and wouldn't even if I could. But I don't want to be reminded of them. What about you?" I say.

I catch her eye again looking for something in my face. "Everyone regrets something. Right? That's life. It all brings us to this moment." I say.

I gesture to the train and speeding scenery. Mel shrugs and takes another swig. "What happened after the app? Did you get sacked." She asks through the burn.

"No, I got promoted." I flash her a wicked smile and then turn away. I can almost hear her brain ticking. One, two, three…

"How?"

"Stocks! Victory, despite its flaws, earned us more money than we ever dreamed of. It was the stepping stone that Egotech needed. Our VR division were already the leaders of innovative technologies. We already had a ton of other highly advanced products that weren't ready for the mainstream markets. Our best was a fully augmentative experience that allowed you to feel the effects of virtual reality with the aid of a pressure-sensitive suit. It was more for military training than anything else but it was far beyond our competitors. Another took you into a virtual world with the aid of a screen, a pill and willingness to succumb, although that one had some drawbacks. But that wasn't close to what I'd been working on for years, they were all byproducts of my one true goal. I surmised that if we could copy the mind, truly capture the essence of a single individual, and store it somewhere else, then gaming would take a whole different turn. We could shoot for the stars and explore different worlds of our making."

I let my fingers flutter down like snowflakes. I can't help it. I've always been a motivational speaker.

"Did you do it? Did you reach the stars?"

I close my eyes momentarily caught in the past. I remember the feeling of the first time. The buzz of excitement, the bubbles of nerves, the crippling anticipation.

When I open my eyes, Mel's shoulders have completely relaxed. Like she's at home having a casual conversation with a friend. They said it couldn't be done. I said it could, and I'm close.

"They said it couldn't be done. The board. It took me the duration of the Victory epidemic to achieve it. But I finally manage to copy the mind of one of my employees."

"Who was it?"

"You ask a lot of questions you know, and you haven't answered a single one of mine. How about I'll answer one of yours and then you can answer one of mine."

She nods. It's a start. A thin opening but it's there to be exploited. The newspaper fan gives me a tentative amount of relief from the heat. Melody unconsciously unbuttons the top of her shirt. A small diamond-studded necklace - the ones that hold photos - dangles just out of view.

"Mine first." She says. "What was the name of the person you copied?"

"It was two actually. Stew and Natalie Brown. They were the first to receive complete copying. Cute really. They both worked in the research division. Married a couple of years, completely in love. A couple of kids." I pick up the teddy again as I remember the boy whom he belonged to. "You know the deal. Anyway. They wanted to have "backups" in case either died. And you know fate has that fucked up thing about tempting her."

"They died?"

"Not both, her, Natalie. Car accident. Stew was beside himself. Came into my office demanding that I give him the copy of Natalie." The newspaper in my hands tightens remembering the encounter.

"You didn't?"

"I couldn't!" The newspaper squeals as I continue to twist it tighter and tighter. "How could I? I didn't have the means to put her into anything."

"You never had a plan? You just copied the mind of a fucking human and you didn't think about where you could put it?" Her voice rises with incredulous. "That's fucked up, man!" Mel says dropping back against the seat. She crosses her arm and sucks air through her teeth.

"Oh, we thought about it, but the program wasn't active yet."

My hands are black with the ink of bad news. The heat is stifling. There's a thin sheen of sweat on Mel's chest too as she leans forward once more.

"What wasn't ready?" The thrum of the train echoes in my head like an angry bee. A constant nagging, like a background noise that won't go away.

"Our pleasure dolls."

This enlists a tiny smirk. She's wasn't expecting that.

"You make sex dolls?" She laughs. It's nice to hear. It's not a pretty laugh like a girl's should be. It's a bit more guttural like a pig fucked a fairy and the resulting off-spring had found my remark funny.

"You bet! Do you know how many guys out there would love a sex doll while playing some Virtual Reality porn? Loads. And Egotech had the capital to build all of that. Some of the greatest minds worked for us in one way, shape, or form over the last twenty years. Egotech bridged the gap in the technological revolution, you know."

"But sex dolls? Come on man! Why not a computer or a…" She searches for the right word. "…robot or something?"

"Sort of the same thing," I smirk. "But more fun." I throw a finger through the hole of my left thumb and fore-finger repeatedly.

"Ah, dude. Too much information."

She looks out the window with disgust. I wonder why that is. Why the mere thought of a sex doll can be so alien to most. When all it is is a play toy for some and can be more to others. A companion when no love will find its way to them because of insecurities, disabilities or social complications.

The outside flashes black as we enter a tunnel. For the moment the scar on her cheek is revealed in the black mirror of the train. She catches my stare and pulls her hair over it again. But it's too late I've seen the deep scarring, the sunken skin surrounding her eye. The eye that's lost its lustre. Only a white orb sits there now. One deadeye looking out at a world equally as dead.

A clap of thunder that rocks the train. Rain lashes the windows in frightening bursts. A silence fills the train with creeping dread. Even though I was expecting it, I can still feel my heart racing. I never did like thunder. Not since I was four and I got caught out under the big oak tree behind my house.

"Did you do it?"

"What?" I ask with confusion.

"Did you do it? Did you put Natalie into one of your dolls?"

"Yes. We tried our best to make one the exact image of Natalie. For Stew's sake. I think we did a great job. Stew even agreed when he saw her. But the difficulty came when we introduced Natalie's copy into the structure of the doll."

"How?"

"You have to remember Natalie was used to using her god given limbs. Integration took a few weeks. We had the best therapist go in and speak with Nat, she understood what had happened, but it was still hard for her. One minute she's dead surrounded by darkness not knowing what her world is and then she's thrust back to reality."

"Damn! That's harsh."

"I agree, but it had to happen. After the treatment, we brought her home. Her sons were waiting eagerly to see their mother again. Stew explained that she would be different but it would still be their mum. I saw the fright in the boy's eyes when we carried her out of the car. The youngest loved his mother unconditionally but the eldest one didn't seem to accept the fact that she was inside the doll."

The weight of the chair catches me as I slump back and watch the green fields blur by. The rain still lashes the glass and the thunder clouds boil above us. Melody has been hanging on my every word. The chain around her neck is now in her hand. The golden locket fumbling from thumb to finger. The half of her face I can see is bright and alert.

"Why are you running, Mel?"

She snaps shut like a clam. Recoils from the question as if burnt.

"Is it from somewhere?" I ask.

She doesn't look.

"Someone?"

Still nothing.

"Something?"

Her shoulders tighten again.

"Ah, something. Something happened that you want to put distance between. I can relate to that."

I gesture around the metal compartment we now sit in. She glances around and nods. She puts her head in her hands and breathes deeply.

"I did something..." She stretches up and wipes her face. I can see the start of a tear in her eye before she bats it away. "...but it wasn't my fault..."

"...Anyway, back to the story." I cut her off. She needs more time. "For the first few days, the family started to return to normal, if you can say normal when a family has a sex doll as a parent." I chuckle then stop realising how bad it makes me feel. I swallow the feeling and bury it with my other past transgressions.

"A few months later Stew comes to my office. He wanted Natalie to have better functions."

"What like sex positions?" Mel's face crinkles with confusion. She's not looking at me even though I know she wants the narrative to continue, she stares transfixed out the window.

"No, not positions. Articulations. Stew wanted her to be able to move. Even if it was just her head, or hands. At that point, Egotech's robotic division was testing a prototype android. Fully functioning. The whole caboodle. I got Stew to bring her in and to tell you what, I was shocked to see the condition of Natalie."

"Your product wasn't user-friendly obviously." She snorts. I hear the smugness in her statement. I can understand it too, but that wasn't it.

"Our product was fine. But it wasn't used to the beating."

"He beat her? His wife?" This enlists the fire I expected. The spark that ignites Mel's wrath.

"That's what we guessed. Stew wasn't saying anything except Natalie had fallen a few times. She couldn't bruise, synthetic skin couldn't, but her skin could scrape and tear. Stew also asked if she could be tighter, you know, downstairs. And if you saw what he meant it would give you nightmares. As a woman I mean."

"What do you mean?"

"Well, he wasn't gentle, let's put it that way. A therapist tried to explain it to me. Stew saw his wife as incapacitated. Although Natalie was inside the doll, he had separated her from it. Treating the body as he wanted. Without any regards for his wife's emotional turmoil. We transferred Natalie into a new bio-body. One with all the functioning of a regular human - apart from bodily. Within the configuration of the android mind we used to house Natalie's consciousness, we allowed for storage of visual and audible feeds. We watched the recorded time span when we transferred her. Some of that time was pretty tough to watch."

I glance at the red booties on the chair beside her. Mel hasn't seen them yet. I wonder what her reaction will be. Another tunnel thunders pass and I snap my eyes up to hers. She shoots me a frightened look and then it vanishes along with the darkness of the tunnel. She takes a long draught of the alcohol and hands it to me. It still seems as full as when we started drinking. I can feel a little buzz. It's nice in a take-the-edge-off way.

"We went through the months of stored footage," I say leaning back closing my eye.

"Even we could see the patches of darkness on 24x speed. Stew spent more time out with friends shutting Natalie away in darkened rooms. The children spent more time with the nanny than their own mother. Even the youngest distanced himself from her. Then there were the times Stew used Natalie for his own gratification. I won't go into that." I smile weakly. "I wouldn't want to hurt your pretty little ears."

She laughs again. Short and barking. "They're far from pretty." The alcohol is having an effect on her too. The frown has loosened, like her shoulders. Maybe a few more and her tongue will do the same. Mel's mouth opens again to speak, but she seems to decide against it and looks over at the window.

"What the hell?"

She picks up the tiny red shoes and waves them angrily at me.

"They're not mine!" I hold my hand up, palms open in a pose of innocence. She inspects the red booties like she's seen them before. A memory probably playing out just behind her eyes.

"I wish you could have seen the look on Stew's face when Natalie came walking out that consultation room."

My grin fills my face, a spit from ear to ear. It was a good moment. One of those one-in-a-million karma smashing moments. When all is set right in the world. Mel doesn't notice. The booties rotate slowly in her hands. Every inch under her scrutinising eye. I let the silence build. We have all the time in the world. This tin can isn't going to stop any time soon. Might as well sit back.

"He killed her didn't he?" She says it abruptly, completely taking me unawares.

"Nope." I groan and sit back up. "They went home, lived happily for a while. Until they tried to kill her. Stew and the many Trisha. They had been having an affair. Trisha was a Jesus freak. Thought our creation was the devil's work. I suppose she was. Stew took a blow torch to Nat, but her survival instinct kicked in. Then she killed him."

"She killed him?" But I thought robots couldn't hurt humans?"

"You're forgetting one thing. The same thing the judge missed."

She looks puzzled for a moment and then realisation sets in. "She wasn't a robot."

"Exactly. Natalie wasn't a full android. She was a consciousness inside a robotic body. She could do whatever she wanted. Stew was found with his man parts burnt off."

"Ah, man. Gross."

"You bet. Sickest thing I've ever seen and I've seen a fair bit of gruesome. Nat tried to run away but thanks to our tracking we caught up with her. Saw the whole thing on the storage. So we wiped it. The police pulled her in and it was her word against Trisha.we convinced the judge that robots couldn't do any harm and Trisha took the fall."

"You lied to the judge?"

"I told a different version of the truth. Nice booties." I say it with a flick of my head indicating the booties.

"Were they always there?" She's scared. I can hear the hint of fear in her voice. "Like, when I sat down. Were they there then?" She pulls at the laces, then almost throws them down and reaches for the flask. I let her take it, she's in more need of it than me.

The heat piles on again. It's relentless. Each wave makes me want to peel another layer of skin off. It's not the tempest raging outside the train. It can't be. Rain, wind, lightning. In this place, they're all cold. Mel flaps the collar of her shirt puffing air in and out. I'm glad it's not just me.

"What happened to Natalie?"

"We don't know. Never found her. No fingerprints see." I waggle my fingers. She laughs and lifts the drink.

"Now It's my turn." The flask stops at her lips. She eyes me, pours, swallows and nods.

"Okay. What you want to know."

"What did you do? Did you hurt someone, a friend, mother, father, boyfriend?"

A tunnel thunders pass again. A flash of black, and then bright, wide eyes seeing the temporal clouds of black spots blinking around the compartment. Mel looks at me with downcast eyes. A look of total hopelessness.

"Ah, still not ready. Let me tell you another tale of one of our technologies that are saving lives."

"Destroying you mean."

"That's a bit unfair. It saved Natalie didn't it?"

"Yeah, after it killed her husband!" She eyes the booties again and then turns so her back is to the window and the red shoes.

"Psst, an oversight. How could we know she was a psycho."

"Ha! You made her one! How would you feel if you were downloaded, shoved into a body that wasn't yours and then tortured?"

"It's just code. I wouldn't feel one way or another."

"It's not just code! It's can't be. We're talking about human consciousness."

"Yes and no…"

She begins to cut me off.

"...it's complicated. The mind is complicated. When we copy a mind, it's not a transference of flesh."

"So what? You're saying you're copying the soul! Are you proclaiming to be gods now?"

"Of course not. More like mediators."

She laughs again. The pig fucked fairy. It's amusing.

"That's unbelievable. You're just putting people into bodies. That serves no purpose for the greater good. I mean, come on!" She throws her hands up in frustration.

"You tell that to a mother holding the hands of her four-year-old son while he's in a coma." My retort has the desired effect.

"Oh my god."

For a moment I wonder why she's so shocked. Did she have a child? Was that why such a reaction to the comatose kid, and the infant's shoes? I try reading her behind the hand at her mouth, but all I see is genuine empathy.

"His name was Toby," I say.

"What happened?"

I glance down at the picture of Toby on the newspaper. His blonde hair has a short quiff across his forehead. The headlines read Boy aged four, mowed down by drunk driver. I hold it up for Mel to see. Her brow furrows like she's seen it before.

"I carry it with me." I swallow past the lump. "To remind me of him."

"Did Toby die?"

She seems generally concerned again. Maybe it's the alcohol adding to her own sense of guilt. We all know how that works. The greenery outside blends to grey with the sheets of rain. It reminds me of the story.

"It was raining. Toby and his mother had just been to the library to get some new books out. One for every day of the week, he would have said." I half-smile.

"The car came out of nowhere, mounted the curb and ploughed little Toby down. The car threw Susan back against the library but Toby got caught under the car. It dragged him twenty feet before it bounced over him and screeched off. I was doing some grocery shopping when I heard the car and saw the impact. I followed to the hospital to see if I could help. When Toby was put on life support I offered Egotech at their disposal. No charge."

"So you do have a heart?" She smirks.

I know she's kidding but it strikes something deep inside me. Did I have a heart?

"The mother was obviously reluctant. But I told her it was just a precaution. We could download his consciousness, even if she didn't want to use it, like a backup. Insurance if you will. She asked some question and I left her with a card. Susan called in the next day wanting to know more. I showed her our profiles, how it worked, what to expect, that sort of thing. Susan was driving for it, I brought the rig, just in case. We connected Toby up. I told her to come to the office the following day to see the upload."

Mel stands to seat herself opposite me, she gently takes the paper out my hand and looks at the image of Toby and his teddy bear. "Not another doll, please no. I couldn't stand a child doll. That's just creepy."

"Not a doll. Don't worry. We didn't want to replace young Toby, just give him a temporary home until he came out of his coma and then we could put him back. It would be like Toby had a few days sleep. He'd be none the wiser."

"So what did you do?"

I search her eyes to see if she can guess. She gasps.

"Not the teddy!"

"Why not! It was perfect, with a few adjustments. Didn't you ever dream about being like your best friend when you were a child? Think about it. Toby has an attachment to the bear, it would be easy for him to wake up in his teddy bear rather than something unfamiliar."

A bolt of lightning crackles down over the landscape filling the gloomy skies with electric blue and purple flashes. It's beautiful in an I'm-not-shitting-myself-way. The darkness closes in in the absence of the flash. The rain drones on.

"Do you know what Toby asked for when we unloaded him to the bear? To read his books."

"Didn't he remember the accident?"

"Clearly not. But we thought it best to tell him any-way. We wanted to have a reason why he couldn't move. It was frustrating for him at first and there were moments that were difficult to handle. He even baulked when Susan came near him. But after a while, I think the ruse worked. Susan was ecstatic she had her little man back. Mean-while, things at the hospital took a more scary turn."

I can see tears welling in her eyes while the silence stretches. The newspaper crinkles in her lap. I take another swig of gin and pass her the flask. She drains the last of it in one long drought.

"Four is such a young age to die." She says.

"He didn't die...hasn't died...yet." I correct myself.

"He's still alive?"

"To this day, yes."

"Is he still in a coma? What could have happened that was so scary?"

"Toby's real parents showed up."

Her jaw physically drops.

"Toby was hurt pretty badly, he was covered with gauze and bandages. So much so that he was covered in them. Even his face. No one thought that Toby wasn't Susan's. Toby, or rather Harry Bank, had been missing for well over six months when a nurse saw a picture of him in the paper."

I point to the newspaper in her lap.

"She called the authorities straight away. The rest, as they say, is history. The police brought me in for questioning. I told them what I knew, what had happened. They made me call Susan to tell her we had an important update for Toby's mainframe. She must have heard something in my voice or saw the broadcasts about Harry Bank."So wait, she stole someone's child and then you copied that child's consciousness and put it in his teddy for her to take away forever?"

"Pretty much. Susan, if that was her real name, disappeared. Gone like a puff of smoke. Now we put tracking within the code, so we know where our products are at any given time. Makes working with the police easier that's for sure."

She sits back, a distant look clouding her eye. She absentmindedly fingered the scar on her cheek. A moment passes and then she locks eyes with me.

"I don't remember getting this."

She pulls her hair out the way. Her left eye is dead. It doesn't move when her other blue eye moves. The deep scar runs from just under the white eye down to the curve of her lip. It's raw, blotchy and red. The stitches are still visible close to the skin, one has opened revealing the weeping wound beneath.

"In truth, I don't remember boarding this train. Since you've been talking I've remembered some...things."

"What do you remember?" I ask gently.

She lets the hair fall and closes her eyes.

"Noise. So much noise. And pain." She winces at the memory.

I wait for the lines on her face to soften as the memories move on.

"It wasn't my fault, the accident. I had to get away."

"It's never our fault when it's the act of desperation, but we should still be held accountable."

I say it with feeling. I know what it feels like to want to disappear rather than fight the demons at your door. But we all have them and we must confront them sooner rather than later and make peace or those demons will eat your soul.

"She wouldn't listen."

"Who wouldn't listen, Mel?

The tears threaten to erupt from her eyes. One escapes and barrels down her cheek. Mel swipes it away angrily and sniffs a few times.

"Julie, my partner."

She brings her sleeve up and dabs at her nose. The tears fall now as another tunnel rumbles past.

"Julie always liked to do drugs on a night out. Nothing heavy. Maybe an E, a bit of coke. She should have said no! But they were all doing it. How could she?"

Now I've got her talking the words tumble out.

"It was like the newest thing on the streets. It was everywhere. I told her to wait. Not to be a guinea pig. But Julie's stubborn. She gets it from her dad. The old Scottish cunt, he doesn't take no for an answer either, just like her. I hate the bastard. He blames me for his precious little daughter being a lesbian. Jokes on him though, because Julie turned me." She laughs again mirthlessly and then breaks down.

"She said it would be ok." She says between the sobs.

"What was it called?

"I don't know, something like the rabbit hole or something."

"Tunnel vision."

"That's it. Who calls a drug tunnel vision? I suppose it was because that's what it felt like. It did to me anyway. When you took the pill it did something to your head so when you looked at a tv screen or phone or anything like a video it took over. It caused you to live in that film. The one on the screen in front of you. It was all shits and giggles in the clubs. All they played was dancing videos with fluffy fucking Unicorn. If you were happy then you had the time of your life. But if you weren't, then it was a different story. One guy Julie knew went out of his way to make it the scariest experiences of his life. He wanted that. He got off on the fright. Fucking madman if you ask me. I wouldn't watch horror films in the day time. Let alone want to live one out."

"So what happened?"

"Julie brought some home. She had an idea that she wanted to try. She lost her mum when she was really young. Brain tumour. She wanted to relive those times with her. Julie rung me up all excited, tells me that's she's got a few of these pills and to get the big screen setup. When she gets home she puts on the video and she pops a pill telling me to come with her. I...I did it. And, and my phone rang."

She breaks down looking at the imaginary phone in her hands.

"My dad called."

"Why was that bad?"

"You've got to understand. Where I come from things are different. People are different. My dad had a farm, no one ever found out what he did. But I did. One morning I woke up alone, no one in the house. I went in search and found him doing...I can't!"

"You must."

"He...wa...he wasn't alone. There were these other people in robes standing around watching as he and this lady...," she shakes her head trying to dislodge the image.

"Then there was a knife." The tears fall unchecked. "He killed her right there on the table, they all did. There all took turns to stab her. I couldn't take it. I packed a few things as quickly as I could and I ran away. That's when I met Julie at the train station. She had run away too."

"What happened when you took the pill?"

"I remember that incident at my dad's farm. The drug wasn't supposed to work like that, but it did. Only this time I was the girl and my father was doing those disgusting things to me. I couldn't move, couldn't run. They held me down while he…"

Mel jumps up and punches the train window, again and again until her hand becomes bloody. The window is smeared with the red of her blood when her anger finally wanes.

"Have you ever been killed?"

I can't help but grimace. I haven't, technically, but it stills feel like it.

"Each time that blade came down I felt the steel bite. Hours and hours of torture. But it never wore off fully. Even when the drug had gone out my system I still saw those images behind my eyes. I had to numb it somehow. There was a bottle of whiskey that Julie had brought at Christmas. I drunk that until I couldn't feel the knives. Until the memory went away."

Another tunnel thunders pass, they are coming quicker now. As is the rain. Thick angry swarms bombard the train in violent bursts.

"When I came to, Julie was there. She told me everything would be ok. But I couldn't shake it off. She enjoyed her trip so much she did it again the next night. I didn't. I sat and drank until I was numb. But I ran out of booze. So I got in my car to go to the shops."

Mel jumps up and paces the train. She grips clumps of hair in frustration. Tears fall unchecked down her face.

"It was raining. The roads were slippery. I remember the girl. I didn't mean to hit her. I lost control.

Slammed on the brakes but it was too late. Next thing I know blood was trickling down my face. I looked up into the rearview mirror and she was laying in the road. She wasn't moving. I got out. Stumbled over to her. There was so much blood."

She looks at the palms of her hand as if she can see the blood still there.

"I killed her! I...ended someone's life." She gasps and buries her face in her hands sobbing.

"I didn't mean to. But I couldn't stay. I took off. I left her for dead."

She continues her pacing never satisfied with the allowed space of the train's compartment.

"WHY AM I HERE?" Her screams pierce my ears.

"Because it's not the first time you've been drunk behind the wheel of a car. Has it?"

She clutches her stomach. The wrath of guilt burrowing deep inside her.

"BUT I COULDN'T GET IT OUT MY HEAD!"

"It's your fault, Mel. No one forced you to drink and drive."

"I didn't mean to, the drink numbed the memories. Stopped them from coming. I had to blackout. It was the only way." She continues to sob as thunder barrels outside the train.

"They picked you up two miles from where you hit poor Harry. You were in a bad state." I point to her face and the dead eye.

"The only reason you haven't been tried for mowing down Harry Bank is that he's still on life support. It's taken six months to get the conviction for the death of Natalie Brown. The lady you killed. We should thank you for that one because if you never crashed into Harry we would never have found you, never found the car that matched the forensic report. So despite you also being dead…"

"What?" Mel wipes the tears in her eye. A horrified expression settles on her face.

"That's right," I say waving my hands around the train compartment.

"This is Egotech's newest product. I call it platform. You, the real you, is on the cold freeze down in the morgue. The judge wanted you to serve the life sentences for the death of Natalie Brown and Harry bank. They're pulling his plug tomorrow, Mel. That's two life sentences for you. I explained to the judge that we could give him what the people demanded even if the eventuality of you never coming out of that coma, which you didn't."

"You can't leave me here! Please don't do this! I didn't mean to!"

Contempt curls on my lip. This is what I've been waiting for. The feeling of self-righteousness. That the world has been set to rights.

"Melody Grace, you will stay in this simulative prison for the duration of your sentence. You won't need to eat, sleep, or anything else but go over and over what you have done."

The edges around me start to fuzz and blur. I lean down and pick up the teddy bear.

"Did I do well Mr Ben?" Asks the teddy bear.

"Yes, Harry. You did brilliantly."

I leave her with a smile as my digital self fades from the carriage.

The screen I'm watching blinks as I take out the USB stick with the digital consciousness of myself on it. It's the only way I could activate Mel's consciousness within the program. A necessary evil. Mel thumps the train glass repeatedly while screaming incoherent things. I stuff the teddy into my top pocket so he can see what I can.

"What now Mr Ben?" Asks Harry.

I glance around the storage facility of Egotech's Neuro-room. The bland grey husks of trillions of terabytes stare back at me. I fold the screen and it collapses on itself then disappears into the column of the Tera-Towers.

"She's our first Harry. There will be more, but as for now, how about a nice game of Victory?"

On my way out I lift the box labelled, "Integration agent," and poke the USB back Inside. We won't need that until the inmates arrive.

About the Authors

In order of story featured

Mark Towse

After a 30-year hiatus, Mark recently gave up a lucrative career in sales to pursue his dream of being a writer. His passion and belief have resulted in pieces in many prestigious magazines, including Flash Fiction Magazine, Raconteur, Breaking Rules Publishing, Books N' Pieces, Artpost, Colp, The Horror Zine, Antipodean SF, Page & Spine, Twenty-Two Twenty-Eight, and Montreal Writes. His work has also appeared twice on The No Sleep Podcast and is set to feature shortly on The Grey Rooms and Centropic Oracle. Seven anthologies to date include his work, two of which are on the 2019 Horror Writers Association recommended list, and a further eight anthologies set for imminent release also contain his work. His first collection, 'Face the Music' will shortly be released by All Things That Matter Press.

Mark resides in Melbourne, Australia with his wife and two children.

https://twitter.com/MarkTowsey12
https://www.facebook.com/mark.towse.75
https://marktowsedarkfiction.wordpress.com/

Kimberly Rei

When Kimberly Rei was five years old, her parents gifted her with a set of Children's Classics that she had no hope of reading. Yet. Sitting at the Christmas tree, surrounded by dozens of beautiful hardcovers, she was giddy with the potential of one day diving into the pages. That love of words and hunger for stories has never wavered.

Kimberly has published more than twenty short stories. Her tales lean creepy and aim to leave you with an unsettling urge to look over your shoulder. She is, like most authors, working on a novel, but an addiction to micro-fiction is keeping her on her literary toes, chasing paper dragons.

Always seeking new ways to make words dance, she has taught workshops and edited novels for Authors You May Recognize.

Kimberly currently lives in Tampa Bay, Florida, with her bladesmith wife, a circle of creative friends, and an abundance of gorgeous beaches to explore. Life is good!

http://tales.studiorei.org/

Michelle River

Michelle has always had a creative spirit and has a passion for painting, photography, pottery and writing. To her husband's dismay, she is happiest when she has three projects on the go, revelling in the chaos around her.

Michelle hails from Ontario, Canada where she is lives with her wonderful husband and fearless daughter. A lover of hot black coffee and everything dark and terrifying, she spends her nights writing horror and dreaming about all things that go bump in the night.

She runs Eerie River Publishing, focusing on promoting indie authors through author services, and publishing a series of high-quality horror and dark fiction anthologies a year.

Follow her adventures in publishing and writing here:

www.EerieRiverPublishing.com
https://twitter.com/EerieRiver
https://twitter.com/MRiver_Writes
www.Facebook.com/EerieRiver/
www.Facebook.com/MichelleRiverAuthor/

Joel R. Hunt

Joel is a writer, proofreader, ex-teacher and part-time human currently residing in the UK. Among his other hobbies of eating, breathing and crouching in dark corners, Joel constantly plans stories and screenplays - a very small number of which actually get written. Most simply languish in his ever-growing 'Unfinished' folder, which is now approaching a mass capable of generating gravitational pull.

Joel's genres of choice are horror and sci-fi, although the odd bit of sentiment does manage to sneak in between the freakishness and disturbing twists. He hopes in time that he might earn a living from putting words on a dead tree in a particular order, or at least earn enough for the occasional cup of tea and vegetarian full English breakfast.

If you are so inclined, you can follow Joel's latest exploits on Twitter, where he also posts daily microstories. But it might be simpler to cut out the middle-man and seek psychiatric help.

https://twitter.com/JoelRHunt1

https://www.reddit.com/r/JRHEvilInc/

https://www.amazon.com/Joel-R.-Hunt/e/B07SBX6G3W

https://www.goodreads.com/author/show/6439719.Joel_Hunt

Tor-Anders Ulven

Tor-Anders Ulven is a father, husband, and horror fiction writer hailing from the cold mountains of Norway. He became known through his horror alter ego hyperobscure, primarily posting short stories on the vast writing subreddit of NoSleep. He has since had work published in several anthologies, and will continue to expand his dark universe for as long as people dare visit it.

https://www.facebook.com/hyperobscure/
https://www.reddit.com/user/hyperobscura
https://twitter.com/hyperobscure

Judith Field

I was born in Liverpool and live in London, UK. I write because it's in my DNA. I'm the daughter of writers and I learned how to agonise over fiction submissions at my mother's (and father's) knee. My father had started writing before I was born, and my mother started when I was about 14. I was encouraged to write as a kid and my father used to set me little writing challenges, then we'd discuss what I'd written. He was a stern critic when I was older.

My short stories, mainly speculative, have appeared in a variety of publications in the USA, UK, Australia New Zealand and, now, Canada. My grandson inspired my first published story when he broke my laptop keyboard. Unlike in the story, a magical creature didn't come out of the laptop and fix my life.

I was Assistant Editor at Gathering Storm Magazine, and Science Fiction Editor at Red Sun Magazine.

I speak five languages and can say "Please publish this story" in all of them. I am also a pharmacist, freelance journalist, editor, medical writer, and indexer. I was awarded an MA in Creative Writing from the Open University in 2018.

https://www.amazon.co.uk/-/e/B00BFS8MFQ
https://www.amazon.com/Judith-Field/e/B00BFS8MFQ?
ref=sr_ntt_srch_lnk_1&qid=1578067838&sr=8-1

K.T. Tate

K.T. Tate is an English author inspired to write speculative fiction. She draws on her love of horror to explore the themes of cosmic and occult horror, the supernatural, folktales and witchcraft. Writing mainly drabbles and short stories, her works have been featured in a plethora of anthologies. All of which can be found on her website below. When not at the beck and call of her monstrous muses she is a geek, enjoying comic books, video games and table-top rpgs.

www.eldritch-hollow.com

https://facebook.com/eldritch-hollow

https://eldritch-hollow.tumblr.com

David Feuling

David Feuling's works have been featured across a number of online and print horror platforms. He is perhaps best known as the author of *The Thing That Stalks the Fields*, which entered the canon of internet horror classics in early 2010. More recently, David has received acclaim for his deep web horror series, *Buyer Beware*, as well as for the standalone short story: *Story of a Mother's Love*.

In 2017, David published an anthology of his shorter works, and also released his first horror novella (*Bravo Juliet*). As of January 2020, David's total collection of works comprises over 225,000 words of published fiction. His current bibliography includes two novels and over 60 short stories.

David currently lives just outside Washington, D.C. with his wife, some friends, and a cat named 笨笨. He holds a bachelor's degree in biology, but doesn't really remember how any of the lab machines work anymore. If you'd like to know more about David's works and latest projects, then you can start by clicking on the following links:

https://www.amazon.com/David-Feuling/e/
https://www.patreon.com/DavidFeuling
https://twitter.com/David_Feuling
https://www.facebook.com/DHFeuling/
The "Simply Scary" Podcast Networks, hosted by Chilling Entertainment
IMDB (writing credit on a 2016 horror short film)
Popular Third Party Anthologies and Community Kickstarter Projects
Reddit's /r/nosleep community
Creepypasta.com
On Youtube (1), (2), (3)

J.M. Smith

J. M. Smith is a stay at home mom from Texas who has always enjoyed writing for fun. After suffering a personal loss in 2018, she was inspired to write what would become her first published story, "A Mother's Certainty". Since then, she has continued writing stories about personal issues, like her son's struggle to speak, in addition to more fun lighthearted stories, like a murderous teddy bear.

She often uses things in her real life as an inspiration for her stories and finds particular pleasure in trying to take ordinary or happy things and twisting them into something darker.

Many of her stories are available in anthologies on Amazon and some can be found on the NoSleep subreddit on reddit.

https://www.amazon.com/Julia-Smith/e/B07RFF19QZ
https://www.facebook.com/jmsmithlikestowrite/
https://twitter.com/JMSmith16246415?s=09
https://www.reddit.com/user/Jullzz15/
https://www.reddit.com/r/JMSmith/
https://jmsmithlikestowrite.wordpress.com/

Grant Hinton

Grant Hinton was born in London, England to two hard-working, unimaginative parents and led a normal life until he found Reddit's Nosleep in 2017. Although a tinkerer of writing since school, Grant hadn't produced anything of note until he took up the horror genre and unleashed a tirade of disturbing stories that have graced Nosleep, podcasts, YouTube videos and incalculable different anthologies out on Amazon.

Grant's stories explore every aspect of horror from technological to good old fashioned demon procession, but mostly Grant likes his writing to wallow around in the depravities of mankind finding that; "Humans are far worse than anything that goes bump in the night and I try to explore that. Although I believe the fight between good and evil is within all of us, people can and have done some pretty fucked up things that monsters and ghosts can't hold a flame to."

https://www.facebook.com/granthintonauthor
https://www.twitter.com/granthinton3
https://www.amazon.com/Wraith-Within-Grant-Hinton/dp/1089062877/

Don't Miss Out!

Sign up for Eerie River Publishing's monthly newsletter to get all the up to date information on new releases, author interviews, book giveaways and so much more.
Sign up for our newsletter here-look

https://mailchi.mp/71e45b6d5880/welcomebook

Looking for additional content?
Becoming an exclusive patron member gives you a chance to be a part of the action as well as gives you creative content every single month, no matter the tier.
Vote on upcoming themes, extra author interview questions, get free eBooks and in the higher tiers get paperbacks sent to you home before they are even released.

Here at Eerie River Publishing, we are focused on providing paid writing opportunities for all indie authors. Outside of our limited drabble collections we put out each year, every single written piece that we publish -including short stories featured in this collection- have been paid for.

https://www.patreon.com/EerieRiverPub